MESSAGE IN THE SKY

JOHN MINICHILLO

Denver, Colorado

Published in the United States by:
Spaceboy Books LLC
1627 Vine Street
Denver, CO 80206
www.readspaceboy.com

Cover art includes creative commons images by macrovector, bs_k1d, and Freepik from Freepik

ISBN: 978-1-951393-26-7
First printed January 2024

Praise for MESSAGE IN THE SKY:

"John Minichillo's *Message In The Sky* is crazy in the best possible way. UFO sightings. Aliens. The Trumps and Clintons - not the politicians, but feuding next door neighbors - become friends and collaborators. I never knew what was going to happen. The novel is a constant, exuberant surprise."

— Marcy Dermansky, author or *Hurricane Girl* and *Very Nice*

"A slyly clever, very funny book... a portrait of America in all its magnificent absurdity."

— Ben Loory, author of *Tales of Falling and Flying*

"You may think you know what John Minichillo is up to when *Message in the Sky* opens, but you don't. Satire, allegory, domestic comedy, universal cautionary tale: there are nods to all of the above, but Minichillo isn't happy to limit himself to just one style. He's too curious and ambitious a writer for that. No matter how fantastic *Message in the Sky* becomes, the world is recognizably ours: technology slams up against the bucolic which collides with the military machine, every page rich with references to American culture and politics. A little Spielberg and a little Peele, Minichillo supersedes genre, with sly wit and compassion, with assured and nimble writing. *Message in the Sky* is both chilling and sweet, and situated in that peculiarly American space of innovation and referentiality."

— Victoria Lancelotta, author of *Ways to Disappear,* winner of the 2022 Catherine Doctorow Innovative Fiction Prize for Katrina

he Trumps and the Clintons were neighbors on Mulberry Court, a winding lane with matching houses, each backyard with a cement patio and a rectangular patch of grass, the yards separated by a privacy fence they sometimes talked over when the mood was right. Tommy Trump grilled steaks as Amy Clinton watched the smoke from his yard fume and rise. Amy imagined the pillar of smoke was a signal that announced them to a helicopter search-and-rescue team, Amy prone to end-times fantasies. Someone would see the signal and come find them, she thought. Though there could be marauders. Perhaps it was best not to announce themselves to the world.

There were lawnmowers buzzing, radios blaring, aboveground pools being splashed around in, but nothing bothered Amy as much as her neighbor's burning of charcoal. She knew it was his right, to grill out on weekends, but she wished he could barbecue without the smoke. He had a method where he soaked wood chips before he added them to the coals, and it made the fire spew a thick cloud that reached high above the neighborhood. Amy marveled at the potency of the smoke that climbed without dispersing. Because here she was, here they all were, breathing it in. She fought the urge to go inside and shower but instead faked a coughing fit to convey her displeasure. Not that Tommy would notice. Not that Tommy would care. Grilling was his thing. So she stayed outside, stubbornly, because she wanted to enjoy the afternoon too, though standing and staring at the fence that separated them only made her angry. Until she became distracted in her thoughts by a strange sound: not a car stereo, not a lawnmower, but a murmuring like a semi truck parked on a distant hill —a low sound like an omnipresent idling diesel. Except in Nappanee there were no hills. And why would a semi park here, in Pleasant Acres?

Amy walked to the fence, looked over, and cleared her throat to let her presence be known. Tommy didn't say anything, so she cleared her throat again, more loudly this time, more obviously *ahem*-ing to be recognized.

"What do you think that is?" Tommy said.

"What *what* is?" Amy said, though she realized she'd been watching it, the source of the sound and like nothing she'd ever witnessed. It was as high as the clouds, and massive and metal.

"It's what it looks like." Amy said.

"I've never seen one." Tommy said.

"I'm not sure we're seeing one now," Amy said.

As if doing so would help them return as quickly as possible to their previously isolated existences, Tommy called for his life-partner, Cherise.

"Cher!" he said. "Come out here! Cher, come quick!"

Not wanting to be outnumbered by the Trumps in their backyard, Amy also yelled for her husband, Jim.

Because of the urgency of their calls, there were two couples, each in their fenced backyards, who stared up at some thing, some *space*-thing that had traveled to them from another solar system or another dimension or another time. It was massive and it hung in the sky, the source of the engine-hum. What was it doing here, above Pleasant Acres, and what did it want from them? Why had it popped the bubble of their domesticity at this moment? Were they up for the challenge it represented—Tommy, Cherise, Amy, and Jim, the Trumps and the Clintons, each trying to enjoy Saturday in their own way but thrust together because of what they saw?

"Get the camera!" Cherise told Tommy.

"Objects in the sky never photograph well," Tommy said. "There's no perspective, so large objects look small."

"It's too far away," Jim agreed, though it seemed kind of close.

"So we're all seeing it?" Amy said, and for the first time she wished there were a gate in the fence that separated the yards. There had never been a reason for a gate, but they should be together for this, or *more* together, at least standing in the same yard. But whose yard, and she knew right away it would be the Trump's yard, that instinctively she and Jim would go over to them and they would accept their coming over as the welcoming neighbors they'd always been. Amy dragged an Adirondack chair over to the fence and stood on it, to look over at the Trumps more freely, and to acknowledge this important moment they were sharing. Tommy looked puzzled by what he saw and Cherise was afraid. Her own husband, Jim, watched the sky with a grim visage of confusion. Amy couldn't quite grasp what this moment meant, but she was sure they wouldn't be smited. This was no War of the Worlds moment, but something that just was, piercing their reality, yes, and who knew for what purpose, but she was quite sure this spaceship wasn't here to kill them.

"Should we call someone?" Amy said.

"Who would we call?" Jim said.

"Who would believe us?" Cherise agreed.

"And what could they do?" Tommy said.

"They could report on it. Write down this day in history. Snap photos with a camera that's better for capturing things in the sky."

Because of the way they lived, the same as everyone around them, Amy had never expected to witness something so real. Except, "real" wasn't the right word. Because it was "unreal." Or maybe it was "real" while the way they lived was "unreal." She was unsure. All she could do was watch.

The object spun on an uneven axis. It reflected sunlight and also glowed orange like an ember. It was angular, like a cube, but it changed shape and at times was more spheroid, or more elliptical. It was hard to gauge how big it was, but it looked as big as the top of a skyscraper lopped off and floating in the air. As if to respond to their doubts and to prove this wasn't some hologram or special effect, a low cloud passed in front of the craft then continued on, the same as it would on any other summer day, though what the small cloud had done, because of what it proved, seemed extraordinary.

"It's just sitting there," Jim said.

Then, as if it were responding to him, the ship spun more rapidly until it glowed an ever brighter orange.

"What's it doing?" Tommy said, but it was obvious. It was doing what they saw. It was becoming more active, for whatever reason, right there in the sky above them.

"It's beautiful," Cherise said, and Amy had to agree. She knew that orange was somehow the opposite of blue, and that this juxtaposition was a nice pairing: orange and blue. Amy tried to remember where she'd seen these colors together, because there were several sports teams who wore orange and blue. The Chicago Bears was one, and a bunch of other teams. Though the Bears' blue was a navy blue, almost black, and their orange was more of a burnt sienna. This orange in the sky was like a hearth, and they stared into its warmth, in awe of what they witnessed, with no words for this collective hallucination. Its spinning slowed, and the shape of the thing became more solid, with a façade-like quality to its surface, like something constructed, if asymmetrical, and there was no visible propulsion system, no reason that it should float in the air.

"Do we still have those eclipse glasses?" Jim said.

He was reaching for a way to make sense of the object because there was nothing to be gained by looking at it through eclipse glasses, which had allowed him to stare at the sun, though Jim believed there was a hidden aspect that would be revealed by simply looking at the thing the right way. The eclipse glasses would only make it harder to see, but Jim wanted to decode the object and the eclipse glasses were the best idea he could come up with in the moment.

"Is anyone else seeing this?!" Cherise shouted for anyone to hear, but there was a stillness in Pleasant Acres, everything quiet except the unsettling low murmur that came from the sky.

"Is anyone out here?!" she shouted.

"Me and Jim are here," Amy said, and she got back up on the Adirondack chair to look over the fence and wave.

"I meant anyone else," Cherise said. "I knew you guys were here."

"Can you believe it?" Amy said. "Can you even believe it?"

"I don't know what to believe," Cherise admitted. She might have been saying she'd never known what to believe, though if she were asked on any other day, she'd have had sure answers about God, family, and the armed forces.

For her part, Amy had been less sure, with her loyalties to family, physics, and pizza.

They knew that this moment would soon end, and what they watched now was the climax. Though they were skeptical about the quality of any photos from their phones, they each took them from their pockets and snapped videos and stills, zooming in on the craft by un-pinching fingers on touch screens, their best attempts to capture the thing as it ended its dance.

There were smaller objects that came from somewhere unseen, maybe from inside the ship. They were balls of light that curlicue-d around the big ship and left dark trails in the bright blue patch of sky. They looped lines in a circuit like a spirograph with quick arcs re-transcribed until dark hieroglyphs became visible, with four distinct symbols, whatever they were, that appeared beside the craft. It was a message for humanity, here to be witnessed in Pleasant Acres, recorded on the photos of the Clintons and the Trumps, in their nearly identical backyards as Tommy's steaks overcooked untended, and the smoke trail from his grill led up to a glowing orange patch of sky that faded as the small scribblers disappeared and the big ship shot away at an unlikely angle and an impossible speed, so that it was gone and all that was left were these neighbors who never really liked each other, dumbfounded and not quite ready to return to their ordinary lives. They wanted to hang on to the moment a little longer and so they repeated to each other over the fence, "What the fuck was that?!"

For weeks, Amy Clinton felt a sense of anxiety whenever she went into the backyard. Tommy Trump had stopped grilling on Saturdays, which was unlike him, and she would stand on the Adirondack chair to peek over the fence, just to make sure he wasn't there. She hoped he was there, so she wouldn't be alone should the ship reappear, but he was never there, like he had decided to rope off this part of his life and never return, something she knew she couldn't do, because she was drawn to the thing, even if it meant death, even if it erased everything she thought she knew about this world. And as she looked up, she tried to remember the peculiar quality of that particular hue of orange and she tried to decide upon a definitive shape for the spacecraft, which she was sure it was, no matter how much Jim doubted his own eyes and tried to talk her out of it.

When she said something about the message in the sky at dinner, Jim said, "Pass the potatoes."

When she said something about the message in the sky in bed, he said, "I'm a man, Amy. We're married. I have needs. When was the last time we've *been* together?"

⅋

And she knew it wasn't that long ago, but he had her suddenly counting backwards, and there was the ship in the sky, as a marker of time in their changed lives moving forward, and he was right, their last intimate embrace had been before that. Jim was trying to go back to the way things had always been, but for her, the object made her feel like an ant. Or a mouse. It was a hawk up there watching them. It hadn't struck last time but what if it came back? She had wanted to talk about it while Jim wanted to ignore the most important day in their puny lives, and Jim wanted sex. She was supposed to have known that, and to be sorry about it, and to remedy the situation with a quickie, even though she was out of sorts and had been since that day.

"What do they want?" she said.

Jim said, "Who?"

"*They*. Them."

"You think it was space aliens?"

"Who else?"

"It could have been a balloon."

"It wasn't a balloon."

"It may have been a mirage. From heat. Light may have reflected off heat waves in the atmosphere."

"It was no mirage."

"Well, there's no such thing as aliens."

"We saw them."

"Whatever it was we saw, we did not see aliens."

"Who do you think was driving?"

"It could be from our own government."

"They can't build an F-22 without spending a trillion dollars. How in the hell would they make something like *that*?"

"But you go right to aliens?"

"And why don't you?"

Jim rolled over so he faced away from her and he quit talking. There wasn't going to be any sex and he was throwing a tantrum. But how could she have sex with someone who was so rigid in his beliefs, who couldn't admit what he'd seen? And while it wasn't why things had initially cooled between them, she saw how maybe this was the new character of their relationship for a while.

"If our government knows," Amy said, "they don't keep it from us because they think we can't handle it. We can. It's because they're afraid we'll make peace all over the world. We'll see the folly of money and war and discover the many ways we can help each other."

"You think space aliens would get rid of money?"

"They wouldn't, but maybe we would."

Jim lay on his back. He still hadn't touched her or looked over at her, but he was opening to Amy.

"There are so many assumptions you've made," he said. "The first of which is that aliens exist."

"I'm willing to make that leap," she said. "It's what makes sense. They were trying to communicate with us."

"With inkblots?"

"They were symbols. It was writing."

"If you want to communicate with a monkey," Jim said, "You don't write on the wall. You give it a banana."

"There are monkeys who can read."

"I don't believe you."

"I saw one on YouTube. She reads pictures on cards and she can arrange the pictures to say things."

"Let me guess: one of the pictures is a banana?"

"She's a very intelligent creature. She takes what they give her and communicates complex emotions."

"It doesn't mean aliens are real."

"I think they're real. And they want us to know they're real."

"So that's the thing," Jim said. "Why would they keep themselves secret for all these years."

"Maybe they haven't," Amy said, "but the TV news has."

"We've seen pictures of flying saucers for decades and they're always fake. One was a pie pan."

"What we saw was not a pie pan."

"No it wasn't."

"So what was it?"

"It wasn't what you're saying," Jim said.

"How can you be sure?"

"I'm sure. They would have had to have come too far. And why would they?"

"Look at this place," Amy said. "Wouldn't you want to live here? Maybe they came from a barren rocky planet. Or a planet that was too hot. Or too cold."

"So they did a drive-by? To check the place out?"

"Maybe what they want is something else," Amy said. "Something we can't even see."

"Why make it complicated?"

"Space travel is complicated."

"You need this to be true," Jim said. "It's like religion for you."

"I didn't ask for this," Amy said. "But here we are. It's exciting."

"There wasn't anything on the news."

"We didn't tell them."

"They'd make us look like kooks."

"We are kooks," Amy said. "But we can't be the only ones."

"They're not going to put us on the news," Jim said.

"So we make our own news."

"And how do we do that?"

"With a website."

"A news website?"

"Just a website. About the writing in the sky."

"And people will see it?"

"Eventually," Amy said. "People will make connections. They'll figure something out about it."

"About the message? If it was a message."

"We have to try."

Jim Clinton did his best to ignore what his wife had become obsessed with, though in their marriage he had learned to never say to her that she was "obsessed" with anything, except that she was more obsessed than he'd ever seen her, so he said it to himself and he knew it was true, which made it harder to be around her because the thing he didn't want to think about was the thing she was always thinking about. He didn't believe it was true, but even if it were true other people had seen strange things and were able to move on with their lives. He even knew how they did so. It was easy. There was work to do, movies to see, holidays to plan for, and all that driving in between. He loved to drive as much as Amy hated to drive and it made them a good pair. When the weather was nice, they drove in the 4-Runner with the sunroof open to the Amish market to get a pie, though now he'd rather have the sunroof closed, since they both thought about the ones up there watching, and he hated to acknowledge the possibility.

"Do you think they chose us?" Amy said.

"Who?"

"You know who. Maybe they've observed us for a long time."

"I'm thinking about pie."

"I'm not going to let you change the subject."

"The coconut crème is my favorite but I'll try something else. How are the Amish getting coconuts anyway? Isn't that cheating?"

"I'm going to ask them if they've seen anything," Amy said.

"Don't."

"They have to have. They live out here in the dark. Without distractions. Surely, the UFOs are curious about them."

"I think curiosity is a human concept."

"It is not," Amy said. "Elephants are curious."

"Elephants are mammals," Jim said.

"Are they?"

"Pretty sure. They give live birth."

"You don't think aliens can be curious?" Amy said.

"I don't think aliens exist," Jim said. "I think we made them up and project our own shit onto them."

"Like those symbols? How am I projecting that? We all saw it."

"We saw something we don't understand. It doesn't mean it was writing."

"It looked like writing."

"Every time we've moved," Jim said, "we've had to get rid of half of our books. Writing is outdated technology and why are aliens going to write to us if they can communicate telepathically?"

"It was so we could show other people. So someone out there would see it and understand. I want you to help me with a website. I don't see why you have to be so stubborn."

"It seems like we'd be exposing ourselves to weirdos."

"So."

"We have a nice life."

"I think this is what we were meant to do," Amy said. "You don't have to believe in it, but I need your help. It would be so easy for you, but I wouldn't know where to start."

"You start with a domain name."

"What should it be?"

"It depends what's taken. You want something people can find and that they will remember."

"Like *UFO-writing-dot-com*?"

"I wouldn't call it 'writing'."

"What would you call it?"

"The message in the sky."

"I like that. Dot com."

"I'd go with dot net," Jim said.

"Why?"

"Just to change it up. Everybody uses dot com. Dot com would seem somehow less serious. You still buy dot com but it redirects to dot net."

"See. You're good at this. Why won't you help me?"

"I'll help you, but when nothing happens don't be disappointed."

"What if something does happen?" Amy said. "Will you admit this is important?"

"I'm always going to love you," Jim said. "But I don't want this to become the focus of our lives. If I make you a website is that going to make things better or worse?"

"In what way?"

"Will you obsess over it?"

"Oh my God," Amy said. "I am not obsessed."

"You seem obsessed."

"Well maybe *you* should be," she said. "We saw what is maybe the biggest event in our lives. Maybe it's the kind of thing that is okay to obsess over."

"But you don't like me saying it?"

"Because I'm not."

"But it would be okay if you did?" Jim said.

"It would be okay. It would be very okay."

"I'll make you a website if you promise not to check it more than twice a day."

"I can't promise that."

"That's reasonable. We can set up alerts so you don't need to check it. I can make it so it sends you a daily report."

"I think I would like checking it. You don't have to do all that."

"It's going to drive you crazy."

"It already has," Amy said. "I need to know what they said. I need to know what that was."

"I don't think we're going to find out."

"So you're open to the idea that it was a message?"

"I don't think it has meaning and that's the main reason I don't think we'll ever uncover a message."

"It had to be a message. What else could it have been?"

"Exhaust? Squid ink? Plasma? Condensation?"

"You can make me a website, and I can check it as much as I like, and I can believe whatever I want to believe."

"I'll do it. But only if it's going to make you happy."

"It's making me happy right now."

"How happy?"

"I think you know."

"Really?" Jim said. "You want to?"

"I will. For the website."

"Deal."

"Okay."

"I want to do it twice," Jim said.

"You already said 'deal'."

"How about tonight and tomorrow?"

"Yes."

"You're saying 'yes'?"

"Yes."

"This is really important to me," Jim said. "I don't want that thing getting between us."

"I know. I'm sorry. I've been preoccupied."

"Preoccupied is a good word," he said. "Instead of 'obsessed,' from now on I'll say 'preoccupied'."

"I'm not preoccupied now."

In a dojo on a military base, Airman Riley sat lotus-style in Air Force issue shorts and a t-shirt as his superior paced in front of him barefoot but otherwise in full dress uniform on the squishy wrestling mat. He peppered the sitting Airman with questions as the recruit attempted to meditate despite the pacing and the verbal distraction. He understood that the questions weren't meant to be answered, but to be meditated on as he went to that place, the one inside that was wide open. Airman Riley could travel anywhere and leave his body behind. It was a talent he'd known since he was a child and the brass somehow found out about him.

"They don't trust us," the Major said. "But they don't understand the threats we face.

"Approach them with a peaceful mind," he said. "Blot out everything around you and try to learn what they want.

"If they know you're one of us, they won't talk to you. We want the technology, but don't want to have to give up our guns to get it."

Airman Riley couldn't blot out his associations with the Air Force because the Major kept talking, but if Riley said anything about it, the Major would talk more. He stretched his back and wiggled his toes to try to better relax as he focused his mind on his mantra, "Carol Pasternak," which he repeated to himself over and over until he no longer heard the Major yammering and Riley was no longer in the dojo, but he moved through a mist toward a hovering spaceship.

Carol Pasternak was not a real person, or at least not anyone he'd ever met. The mantra was really just a collection of syllables that was given to him by a Tibetan monk when he wandered the Himalayas at night instead of sleeping, as his body remained reclined in his parents' house, in his old bedroom. The monk didn't speak English but they understood each other, and Riley suspected the mantra was ancient, and that it meant something, but the mantra sounded close enough to "Carol Pasternak" that that's how he remembered it, and saying "Carol Pasternak" to himself over and over was powerful. With the mantra he could travel at will.

"Find out what they're doing. Find out who else knows. We need names and addresses. We need to know what they know. Because if they give away technology to civilians, as we suspect they may, then we'll have a national security emergency like no other. Like any and every Call-of-Duty-playing fifteen-year-old could make nukes out of baking soda and two-liter bottles. We need to keep a lid on that. And we need that for ourselves. Like right now. Like yesterday. Can you see them?"

Airman Riley approached the craft as it hovered eye-level above the mist. This was a large saucer that was maybe sixty feet across, and it bobbed and hummed. He sensed an energy field that prevented him from approaching nearer. He looked down and saw that he was still wearing the Air Force t-shirt, so he wasn't going to be fooling anyone. He waited for a sign from the craft and the craft continued to bob and hum. He held up a peace sign, a door opened, and he was able to walk inside the ship on a path of light that extended to him.

There were three short beings, each in silver jumpsuits. One looked at the elongated fingers on his own hand and tried to repeat the gesture Riley had flashed at them. A second alien motioned for Airman Riley to take the control panel and fly the ship. There were indentations that matched the long six-fingered hands, which Riley was sure his wouldn't fit, but he placed his palm there and the saucer responded. He could feel his presence everywhere in the UFO and while he couldn't tell quite how it worked, he was able to make the ship go where he wanted.

The door was still open, and that was his first command, to shut the door. Because he could still hear the Major talking:

"Have they tried to dismantle our nuclear arsenal?"

"Carol Pasternak. Carol Pasternak."

"Do they have bases under the ocean? Bases in Antarctica? Bases on the far side of the moon?"

"Carol Pasternak."

Airman Riley took off in the ship and he flew as far from the Major's voice as he could, until everything was quiet, in deep dark space. He thought of all the places he could fly: into a volcano, to the bottom of the sea, above Mount Everest, into the eye of a hurricane. But instead he decided to fly to Indiana, where his mom had grown up and his cousins still lived. He wanted them to see this saucer. He wanted them to feel like they were the weird ones for once, because the things he had told them about were true.

He would write his name in the sky for them, RILY, which was how they'd spelled it, because they were dumb and didn't care enough to be right about the small things, and RILY had been a small thing they hadn't thought about in a long time. They knew vaguely that he'd joined the Army, which was what everyone did, except for their cousin Melissa, who went to school and became a nurse, and now when any of them was sick they called her up and she told them all the same thing, to go to the doctor. RILY didn't know if he had to write the letters mirrored and backwards or not, and as he imagined what he wanted the ship to do, he got confused and the letters came out wrong. There was no way anyone would see those symbols and know it was him, so he'd failed again, and maybe his cousins were right. Maybe he really was the weird one.

Cher was alone in the house when she had a notion to look out the window into the backyard. She wasn't afraid of the visitors like Tommy and over the years she'd learned to give in to her impulses. In the bedroom she opened the curtains to see her neighbor, Amy Clinton, meditating on a patch of grass behind the carport. Tommy was nowhere in sight, but she decided he must be involved. If Tommy had put her up to this, or if she suggested it and he agreed, then maybe he was overcoming his fear.

"But why *our* yard?" Cher wondered.

She saw a shovel and wheelbarrow and several bags of mulch and it seemed there was more that was about to happen than Amy meditating. Cher remembered how Amy had acted when Cher had said, "I want to start meditating. I hear it's very relaxing." This was a few years back. They'd had wine and some of Tommy's barbecued beef out on the back patio. The things she was saying weren't really serious, but Amy had to go and act like the expert.

"Stimulating," was what Amy had said, but Cher disagreed. She didn't like being corrected, even about the things she didn't understand, and she clung to her idea of meditation where she thought of it as being relaxing, like taking a nap while awake. Tommy had told Cher that Amy's husband, Jim, was making a website for Amy. She wanted something like that for herself, though Amy had beaten her to the UFO idea, which was the most interesting thing to happen in years. So what could her own website be about? Even if getting a website felt like copying, she wished Tommy would do something like that for her. She decided she would meditate on what her website could be until an answer came.

Luckily, she was already dressed for it, since although she had never done yoga, brightly printed and expensive yoga pants was what she most often wore around the house. She kicked off her cross trainers, got in the middle of the bed, faced Amy in the backyard, pulled her legs together in a torturous full lotus and she sat up straight and hummed to herself, "What can Tommy give me? What do I desire? What can he do for me?"

This was neither relaxing nor stimulating and she couldn't think of anything Tommy could help her with. She chanted with more effort until her hands were balled into fists and she opened her eyes spitefully to see that Amy was no longer meditating but Tommy turned over the grass with the shovel where they were apparently going to plant something. Amy brought over lots of small seedlings for what was obviously going to be a garden. Cher was furious and relieved at the same time, because as soon as she understood it, she knew that a garden was exactly what she wanted and there was Tommy turning over the dirt for her. So meditation really worked. This was amazing, and she saw why so many people made a daily practice of it. Except what was Amy doing there? What did Amy have to do with what she wanted? But then, she understood that Tommy knew nothing about gardening, and Amy was there to teach him, so that he was better able to give this to her. She closed her eyes again and wondered what else she wanted.

"What else do I want?" she said. "What else can Tommy give me?"

And she knew right away that what she wanted was more yoga pants. Now that she had a reason for wearing them, she would need more of them, and she imagined opening packages that came in the mail with yoga pants printed in newer and more modern designs. She could feel the energy from the new pants beginning in her legs, traveling up her core, and igniting in her mind. There was nothing she couldn't accomplish if she meditated over it in some really nice, expensive yoga pants. She might even wear them around town, though that was going to require toning her glutes. So she would also need a top-of-the-line stationary spin bike and at least six weeks. She would debut her glutes around the same time they had fresh veggies from her garden. Maybe her website would be about exercising and eating right. Sure, there were a lot of those, but none were quite the way she would do it. She was a unique individual who was still discovering her talents, and that bitch Amy could have her UFO website because no one important believed in that stuff anyway. With that thought she had come to the close of her meditation session and since she didn't know how else to properly end it she said "Amen" and touched herself in the sign of the cross: on the forehead, the belly, and above each of her breasts that were still perky after all these years and she was glad they weren't as big as Amy's. She got off the bed and had decided to go out back to take inventory of her new garden when she saw Amy bent over and planting a seedling, with Tommy paying special attention to what was nearly falling out of her t-shirt. It was fine, Cher decided. He was human. Even so, she went out there as quickly as she could, agitated and jealous, so that whatever calming effect her first meditation session had had, it had quickly worn off.

"What are we doing, guys?" she said, and Tommy and Amy sat up as if they'd been caught.

"I'm going vegetarian," Tommy said. "It will make me seem better to them up there. Something they can respect."

"Is that so?" Cher said, no longer shocked at what came from Tommy's mouth, except that he was the guy who prided himself on his cookouts, so this was a true reversal of who he'd always been.

"No promises," he said. "But I'm going to try."

"You can do it," Amy said, and this sounded so much like what the trainers at the gym said that Cher wanted to vomit. Amy was making vegetarianism sound like some kind of physical activity and that was so irresponsible, because where was he going to get protein? She'd ask Tommy later when they were alone, and while she was sure he hadn't thought it through, she was mostly concerned for herself, because she wasn't about to give up meat, not even if some UFO didn't like her because of it.

"She told you this?" Cher said. "About the UFO?"

"I came to that conclusion on my own," Tommy said.

"Though I offered to help with the garden," Amy said.

"Look at this!" Tommy said. "Ain't it great?!"

It was great. And now that Amy was sitting up and her tits were no longer hanging out, Cher remembered to be grateful. "Thank you, Amy," she said. "It really is wonderful."

At noon on the solstice, as the sunbeam strikes the temple and the harvest god awakens, the high priest exits the pyramid to address the crowd below. He is a shaman and he has fasted and eaten the herbs that turn his stomach. He vomited through the night and the morning, but the harvest god does not want him to die. The shadow from the pyramid shrinks and moves to the foot of the stairs. In less than a minute the sun will be directly overhead, the pyramid will cast no shadow, and the high priest will speak with the authority of the harvest god. In a wave, the crowd of people kneels and they look up, past him, at something else in the sky. The high priest, also looking up, is overcome with fear, but he remains standing as his knees buckle and he transfers his weight to his staff that supports him. The saucer is large and surrounded by an orange glow. Thimble-shaped objects of light dance around the craft and hieroglyphs appear. Anyone who can read can see what it says, but the high priest has another vantage point and to him the dark blots have a different appearance. He is saddened by what he sees, but how could he have expected anything else? The ruling class has remained indulgent, despite the drought, and a sacrifice is warranted. The small thimble-like craft disperse and disappear in an instant. The large craft spins, pulses, wobbles, and also flies off and is gone.

No one can believe what they've seen, but they're uplifted by the message that was written in the sky, and the crowd emits a joyous roar as everyone gets up and embraces each other, intoxicated by this interlude from the gods. Everyone is happy, relieved of their dearth and buoyant with the gift of life. Until the high priest speaks. What he has seen weighs heavily. He despairs that the gods have chosen him to be the instrument of their unending wrath, and he shouts to the people below. As his voice echoes out from the pyramid, he's alienated from himself, as if it isn't his own voice that he hears, and though he will obey the will of the gods, it will be as if his arms are no longer his own. And he will thank the skies and he will dare to ask for mercy, in the hope that this time they'll be sated.

"The gods demand a sacrifice!" he says. "A child!" He's embellished that last part, but experience has taught him that a sacrifice fights back and a child's at least easier to manage. No matter what anyone might think of a sacrifice, everyone in the community mourns the death of a child. So it will be a child and he'll fast and pray until a peasant name comes to him. He always hears the name of one of the ruling families first, but on that point he'll explain to the gods that they must reconsider. He didn't choose to become high priest and it's a calling he doesn't take lightly. He's also not stupid and he knows the repercussions that would come if he ever suggested the sacrifice of one of the rich kids—to the end of religion and of civilization itself.

And so the people pick up their straw mats and they try to celebrate this solstice the same as any other, despite the message they know they'd seen and the odd proclamation that was made to the contrary. There's no winning for the poor. They have a saying along those lines. There's even a joke where a ruler, a priest, and a poor man all go walking in the woods. The poor man is the only one who knows how to keep them alive outside the city, but in their greed and their ignorance the ruler and the priest betray the poor man and kill him for his meager food, happy with themselves and their full bellies if only for a day.

Each considers hiding the children, or running away. Each has fretted over every new pregnancy. Each has known that without the armed guard and a fear of the gods they could storm the rich and share the bounty amongst themselves, an easily achieved action, so simple yet so absolutely impossible. The feast is humble this year but their prayers are bold.

They say, "Let the rich die of a disease that passes like money from one to the next."

"Let them go blind so we can sacrifice a piglet instead of a child."

"Let them dream of our lives in dirt so they know what it's like for us."

They say, "Return again, and don't let them misinterpret your message of peace."

They say, "Let *them* starve for once."

"Let them choke on elegant foods."

"Banish them."

And they say, "Please, oh great gods, whatever it takes, let them finally come to their senses."

In bed, on her laptop, with Tommy beside her and The Tonight Show on the mounted flat-screen TV, Cher browsed Amy's website that had gone live, and she was impressed with what Jim had done. She wanted her own website, so Tommy was going to have to hire him. There on the front page was one of Cher's photos of the object, a bright metallic box, the photo without attribution. The symbols in the sky had been outlined to give them form, and Cher wondered aloud, "Does this really have to be a message?"

Tommy said, "What?"

"From the UFO. If they're so advanced why don't they land and give it to us in English? Or speak into our minds or something?"

"How do you know they didn't?"

"If they spoke into my mind," Cher said, "I didn't hear a damn thing."

"Maybe you weren't listening."

"But Amy was listening?"

"Maybe that's where she got the idea to make the website." Tommy said.

Cher said, "Maybe they said we owe them forty-five trillion dollars for fucking up the planet?"

"Like the UFO people take dollars?"

"You know what I mean," Cher said. "Maybe they're pissed."

"They might be pissed."

"Aren't you hungry?" Cher said. "You ate nothing but celery and cucumbers. I ate half a chicken and I'm still starving."

"I was hungry but it goes away. If you don't think about it."

"What do you think about?"

"I think about nothing."

"Is that possible?"

"Of course it's possible," Tommy said.

"Isn't your mind racing?"

"It is, at first, but you let it flow through you."

Cher said, "That sounds like Amy talking."

"I've learned some things from Amy."

"What kinds of things?"

"How to quiet my mind. How to be less afraid. How to enjoy the moment."

"You've been meditating?!" Cher said. "Me too! I'm really good at it!"

"You should ask her for tips," Tommy said. "Apparently, you can do it wrong."

"I am not doing it wrong," Cher said. "It totally works."

"Then you know what I'm saying: I think about nothing."

"No, I think about things," Cher said. "Like what I want. And then I get what I want."

"That's not meditating."

"It is."

Cher, who moments ago was happy for their neighbor, Amy, because her website looked professional, was now jealous and upset. She stared angrily at the bedroom curtain because she knew Tommy and Amy's new garden was just beyond it in the backyard, also the site of Tommy's meditation lesson, and who knew how much flirtation.

"You think about more than nothing when Amy's around."

"What's that supposed to mean?"

"I think you know what it means."

"Cher," Tommy said, and he rolled over toward her. "You're the only one for me."

"No," Cher said, "get off of me. We are not doing this right now. I don't know who you are anymore, talking about thinking about nothing."

"I can show you," Tommy said. "Close your eyes."

"They're closed."

"If an idea comes into your mind, just let it go. If another one comes, don't linger on it, let that one go too."

"I have way too many thoughts."

"Try it."

"…"

And Tommy knew he'd gotten through to her because the grimace on her face relaxed. She wasn't smiling, but given time, she might.

"I can't do this with you watching."

"You *are* doing it," Tommy said. "Technically, you should be sitting up, but you feel better, right? Your anger is gone."

"I liked how I did it better."

"This is good," Tommy said. "Try it every now and then and you'll see it makes a difference."

"I still want to eat chicken."

"No one said you had to give up chicken."

"Amy said the UFO people did."

"She doesn't know," Tommy said. "It's just how I feel. It's my truth."

"I want a website."

"What kind of website?"

"I don't know. Can you talk to Jim about making me one?"

"He's busy. I can't ask him that."

"Pay him. Ask what he wants and pay him double."

"They could use the money."

"Of course they could. And we can afford it. Otherwise, what good is money?"

"I'll talk to him," Tommy said, and he tried to maneuver on top of her again.

"Not until you talk to him," Cher said, and she pushed him away to rebuff his advances. "I'm still angry. Use your salesmanship and maybe I'll feel better about you."

The first email that came to Amy's website was a "cease and desist" letter from MessageInTheSky.com. Jim hadn't checked to see if anyone owned that URL before he purchased MessageInTheSky.net, and when he tried to set up the redirect from MessageInTheSky.com, he learned someone did own it, but he decided not to tell Amy. She was anxious enough about her website launch that he didn't think it was information that would have been helpful. He mostly didn't want to have to deal with it. So there was this email now and Amy had to deal with it. The email hadn't come from a lawyer, however, and she was pretty sure she hadn't done anything wrong. Two websites could have the same name. There was nothing illegal about that.

Except the guy, who was a farmer and a pilot who ran a skywriting business two states over, seemed to believe that her UFO website, because of its content, was the equivalent of libel. Amy knew the way to smooth things over was to get him on the phone because she got the feeling he was mostly upset because he thought he was being made fun of. His name was Arnold "Arnie" Fishman and he was available for crop dusting, skywriting, and barnstorming. Amy couldn't imagine there was too much need for barnstorming, so it was the first thing she asked about, before she explained who she was.

Arnie admitted that he'd never been hired to do any barnstorming but he had a barn that was perfect for it and he considered himself well practiced. He said he performed the maneuver at least once a week.

"I really am curious about it," Amy said, "but I should tell you I'm the woman who runs MessageInTheSky.net."

"You're the dot net?"

"My husband made the website. I wanted the dot com."

"I'm not selling the dot com."

"I'm okay with the dot net," she said. "I just want to apologize for any confusion. We didn't know about your website."

"So you're taking it down?"

"I don't think our websites are mutually exclusive."

"They have the same name."

"Did you look at ours?" Amy said. "Did you read it?"

"UFOs."

"They performed skywriting. They did what you do."

"I didn't realize."

"So I have questions."

"I don't believe in UFOs and I think you're full of malarkey."

"My questions are with regard to skywriting."

"Shoot."

"If I sent you pictures of some foreign-looking letters, do you think you could reproduce them? In the sky?"

"Maybe. The letters can be loopy or they can be blocky, but that's about it."

"I'd say more loopy than blocky, but there are some straight lines in there. Are you near a computer? Can you take a look? Click on the menu and there are some close-ups."

"Where's the menu?"

"It's that button in the top-left corner."

"*That's* what that is?"

"Click on it. Do you see the letters?"

"I can do these," Arnie said. "I have to say, though, for an advanced civilization this is not very professional skywriting."

"What's wrong with it?"

"They're not flat. They're going to look like inkblots once the smoke dissipates."

"What kind of smoke do you think that was?" Amy said.

"That might not be smoke," Arnie admitted.

"What else could it be?" Amy said.

"It looks solid. It's reflective. Like metal."

"You think it's metal?"

"It can't be metal."

"But you could do those letters? If we hired you?"

"I don't see what the point is," Arnie said. "If no one can read it."

"It could mean something we don't understand."

"I'm not cheap," Arnie said. "Have you seen my rates?"

"Would you do it in exchange for my husband redesigning your website?"

"He does have a knack for a good-looking website."

"You could use an update."

"I'm going to say 'yes,' but I'll need more details."

"We really did see this. It was real. There's something very important happening, Arnie, and you can be a part of it."

When Jim got home Amy called to him from the bedroom. She was naked and in bed.

She pointed at her naked self and said, "You have to make that guy a website or this isn't happening."

"What guy?"

"MessageInTheSky.com?"

"Oh."

"You didn't think I would find out?"

"I didn't think it was important."

"He threatened to sue us. He thought we were trying to ruin his reputation."

"I don't see that at all."

"I fixed it. But you're updating his website and if you want this to happen, you need to hurry it up."

"I do. But I."

"You're fixing his website."

"Okay, but Tommy hired me to make one for Cherise. There are some things I still need to do with yours. I'm going to be stretched thin."

"This is something we can't ignore. Do you know the odds of a skywriter contacting me out of the blue?"

"Your website is called *Message in the Sky*."

"He can barnstorm."

"How does that help us?"

"We spread the message. We won't even have to pay him. All you have to do is work on his website."

"But *you're* paying me? Like this?"

"Only if you hurry."

"Some people might look at a woman using sex to get what she wants as manipulative."

"Do you want to be manipulated?"

"I do."

"Then quit talking and get in bed."

There were explanations other than extra-terrestrial pilots that would help Jim Clinton make sense of what he'd seen. Except, that he wasn't open to the possibilities. For example, if there were a story about a saucer crash on July 4, 1947, in New Mexico, and it was repeated enough, and the people who believed this story were sincere in their retellings, the lore of this crash would take on a life of its own and it would exist by being retold. It's not a Jim Clinton way of seeing the world, but the events that inspired those stories could be made real by the stories passed down, whether they'd happened or not. Jim Clinton knew where he stood on the age-old philosophical debate: was reality separate from consciousness, or was reality *created* by consciousness? Was a boulder only a boulder when someone perceived it? Or did a boulder exist in some other state of being until recognized? And then, once seen, did the boulder have a consciousness of its own? It may or may not have mass. It may or may not exist on the material plane. It may be that the perceiving of the boulder snaps it into our shared reality. And our not perceiving it hides it away somewhere, where it remains a vibration, or the idea of a boulder. So that the idea of Roswell, if willed into being by conscious minds, has become the reality of Roswell. A past that did not exist could one day exist because of the belief in its existence, and the memories weren't misremembered, but they were made real.

Jim Clinton, however, was a boulder-is–always-there kind of guy. He had faith that his perception of the boulder had nothing to do with the reality of the boulder, which made the world he inhabited different from the way Amy, Tommy, and increasingly, Cher were more open with regard to the nature of the material plane. Whether or not they'd always believed that a spacecraft could blip in and out of perception, they did now.

Was Jim open to the idea of other dimensions? Could this explain things? In so much as "dimensions" was a mathematical concept, he understood that additional dimensions could exist for a computer, but he was not a computer, and he needed to be able to see it. Hadn't he seen the UFO? He had. But he hadn't allowed the vision into his reality in the same way he would a basketball score, a grocery list, or an airline departures schedule. These were abstract representations of real experiences and what hadn't been admitted with respect to the UFO for Jim Clinton was that it was real. He saw something he couldn't explain, and what was required of him before he could understand that was a tearing down of one version of the world to allow for another. Cher hadn't quite put the pieces together yet, while Tommy was excited but frightened about all that it meant, and Amy was downright ready for whatever new world might soon exist.

Amy was pushed beyond what was reasonable in her desire to leap into the unknown. Buying the neighbors a garden, when they were the ones with the money, might still be reasonable, while going out there at night and digging everything up to rearrange it, most definitely was not. Amy didn't know she was right outside the Trump's bedroom and that they might have seen her out there with a spade and a flashlight, undoing what she and Tommy had done, and possibly killing the seedlings, all because she'd spent a few hours on a website dedicated to crop circles, elaborate designs that had appeared in the wheat fields of England for decades. Some carried coded messages and of course this was of great interest to Amy, who had witnessed a coded message of her own.

The dirt was soft and she scooped each plant out and placed them along three lines to form an "H." She soon realized that the tomato plants, with their vine stakes, were going to be much more difficult to move and she remembered that Tommy had pounded in the stakes with a rubber mallet. So she had to rethink the layout of her message. She realized she could move her "H" to the other side of the plot and that the tomato stakes could each represent a lower-case "L." She moved quickly, energized by the understanding that leaving the tomato plants where they were was going to save a lot of time, and before long—though not without breaking a sweat, and while getting her clothes, hands, and face thoroughly soiled—she had spelled out "H-E-L-L-O."

A brown sedan with government plates that gave it away as an unmarked police car crept up the drive to the park ranger's house. Ranger Nelson saw them coming and he stepped out onto the porch to greet them. They wore suits and the bottoms of their slacks were muddied, so they'd been tramping about.

They flashed FBI badges and Ranger Nelson was perturbed that they would come out to his home after hours instead of going to the ranger station at the front gate like everyone else. He was also dismayed that they'd taken this long to get back to him. There had been eighteen missing person's cases in six years and he'd been the one to head up the search teams and field the phone calls. In all that time the FBI hadn't been at all helpful or forthcoming. His own personal theory was pot fields somewhere off the trails and anyone who wandered too close might befall an accident. He had no proof of this, but he mostly stuck to the trails as a result. What he told family members was that it was dark, there was often no cell phone coverage, and the wild woods were disorienting, so that accidents did happen. What the locals said was that they'd seen lights and the missing hikers had been spirited off in UFOs.

The first of the dark-haired agents looked at a park map as he circled around the ranger's house.

"There's an electrical outlet over here, right?"

"One in front and one in back."

"There's a campsite over yonder?"

"About two hundred feet. Just past the trees."

"Hypothetically, we could run an extension cord and power some lights?"

"Hypothetically."

"Could you locate some of the other power outlets throughout the park?"

"They follow the main road. Anywhere else inside the park and you're on your own."

"If we had a generator, people would probably hear that?"

"If there were people to hear. What are you boys up to anyway?"

"We're investigating."

"We can't say."

"But a power outlet is sometimes useful to our work."

"Tell me if any of these names sound familiar," the ranger said. "Heff Younger, Greg Abell, Martin Martinez, Jerry Fitzpatrick, Carl Loebel?"

One of the agents tried to hide the glimmer of recognition while the other busied himself by making notations on the park map with a pencil.

"Should they be familiar?"

"Missing persons cases. All still open. Last seen in this park."

"One of them does ring a bell," the agent with the map said as he looked up.

"I think most of them were found," the other agent said. "There's all this panic because someone was missing when really they simply didn't tell anyone where they went."

"The cases are still open."

"I don't think so. But I'll look into it."

"You will?"

"I said I would."

"If what you need doesn't require too much juice you can use batteries and you can hook them to a solar cell so they charge during the day. If it's daylight you can tap a second solar cell and run directly from that."

"You have those?"

"I do, but they're not cheap. You can buy one at the Bass Pro Shop."

"What size battery?"

"Any size, if you give it long enough to charge."

"Have you seen lights?"

"I've heard stories."

"Not a believer?"

"I work days."

"So do we," the one with the map said, but he was lying. Ranger Nelson could spot a liar a mile off and these guys lied as often as they didn't.

"Will be dark soon," the ranger said. "Time to call it a day," and he went back inside.

When a website went up with language that described a UFO encounter, web crawlers tagged it for review. It was okay to write about UFOs. It was okay to post videos and photos of UFOs so long as there was no high-definition footage of the entities themselves, nor any scientific analyses of energy systems, telepathic communiqués, origin stories, or ultimatums for peace. Making a general call for interpretations of an alleged message in the sky triggered enough alarms that the website, its authors, and any visitors were likely to become the targets of electronic surveillance. It didn't warrant a visit from a field officer or a denial of service attack, but viruses played middlemen and watched for updates. For example, the Clinton's emails, and those of their contacts, were scanned for key words and batched in a case file.

What does fear manifest? There was a change in these neighbors—as evidenced by their text messages, transcribed phone calls, and emails—and Jim Clinton's profile, as the one who owned the website, made him a candidate for some pushback. At first he thought he'd had night terrors. He was paralyzed, hallucinating, and carried into the back of a step-van, with a fog machine spuming in the yard, dwarves in rubber masks running about, and lots of flashing lights. He slept so soundly he felt drugged, as electromagnetic frequencies and subsonic waves kept him disoriented, dizzy, and seasick.

"Where are you taking me?" he said.

"We are from Zeta Reticuli."

"Where are we going?"

"Your discomfort is for the greater good. We are a logical species interested in research. Fear not. You will not remember any of this."

But remember he did.

They took fluids and performed biopsies. They poked and prodded. They turned up the trance music and got in his face. They put a towel in his mouth to keep him from calling for help and they restrained him at the wrists and ankles with plastic cable ties. They spoke to him in mumbo jumbo and pulled facts from his file to give him the impression that he'd been abducted throughout his life, and they'd been interested in him for a very long time.

Before he was in the Air Force, Riley called what he was able to do "walking about." It was the nearest approximation of the experience and required a similar balance of effort and ease. His travels were limited and tired him out, but while he was out there he could explore. They had different names for his ability in the Air Force.

There were code names, project names, and classifications. While no one expressly forbade him from doing so, he was discouraged from "walking about" without the supervision of the Major, since he might stumble upon top-secret information above his grade. He was doing something top secret, for top-secret purposes, but he wasn't necessarily cleared to know about all the things he experienced. He wasn't really curious about what else might be going on, but he'd developed the habit of "walking about." It was his pastime and he didn't really want to quit just because he was being paid. He felt he should be allowed the same freedoms as Michael Jordan, who, when he was the top NBA athlete, had a "for the love of the game" clause in his contract that meant he was allowed to play basketball wherever and whenever he wanted, because the irony for some pro athletes was that once they were being paid, the owners had full control of when and where they played. Riley, who was young and single, with a lot of time and discretionary income, probably should have gone into town to drink or to try to meet girls. Instead he went into town to rent a hotel room where he meditated on the bed until he was free of the vessel of his body and he could roam.

Today, while remembering past explorations, he was drawn to a town in Indiana where he sensed that he was somehow related to the source of someone's extreme anxiety. While walking about in Indiana he saw Air Force personnel impersonating extraterrestrials in order to brainwash and torture some poor man, and this was the end of Riley's keeping neutral. Because one drawback of his gift, as he'd come to discover over the years, was that he either had to use it for good, or suffer karmic consequences. And now that he knew someone was suffering needlessly as a result of an offshoot of the program that had made him wealthy, he had to do something.

Ranger Nelson *had* seen lights. Did the marijuana drug lords have some kind of disco helicopter? He doubted it. Did they come and go at night? Probably. Were there mundane explanations for the things people'd said they'd seen? Maybe.

He carried a Glock that was issued from the park service. Because as the occasional lone arm of the law, he might one day need to draw upon the respect that it commanded while un-holstered, though he wasn't about to go walking into any grow operation. There were other federal agencies better equipped for that kind of thing. And he wasn't stupid. People had disappeared. Experienced campers and hikers had gone missing, with no evidence that they'd wandered off the trail and no signs of a fight. In fact, the more he looked into it, he discovered that the missing persons were all skillful hikers, sometimes with distinction.

He remembered a phone call with the daughter of one such hiker, Becky Lansford, and she said her father could only go a few months at his city job before he needed to get back into the woods. A few days in the Smokies was nothing for him. He'd hiked through jungles and deserts. He'd hiked in Alaska. It just didn't make sense. And the FBI couldn't be bothered to spend more than a day out there looking for him. The agents who'd come out recently, they'd been interested in something else. They were aware of the missing persons but they weren't looking. All they seemed to want was somewhere they could plug in.

Arnie Fishman fired up his yellow biplane and taxied from his barn to the dirt airstrip. He throttled up and the plane rattled and roared until he lifted above the trees and turned to fly the four hundred miles to his destination in Northern Indiana. It was the Fourth of July, so there was less air traffic, but there were boats on lakes and if he didn't make it back before dusk there would be bright bursts of light near the ground all the way home. The job was to fly in over the high school football stadium where Nappanee held their fireworks celebration. With everyone oriented toward that patch of sky in anticipation of the rockets' red glare,

Arnie would perform the twisted loops to write out as near a copy of the UFO message as he could manage. He wouldn't hear anyone, but he supposed there would be "oohs" and "aahs," the same as for the fireworks, except that when Arnie was done and he had flown back on his way, there'd be nothing but confusion. Because what did it spell? What did it mean?

Amy Clinton didn't care that no one would understand. Maybe the message wasn't for them. On one level it was. If this was an ancient phrase that would awaken humanity, then so be it. Mostly, she was sending a message to them up there. To see if they were watching.

Was mimicry a sign of intelligence? Not necessarily. But she was letting them know that she'd paid attention and she was open to further communication.

Amy took off her gardener's hat and she waved it at Arnie, who couldn't see her, had never met her, but was really happy with what Jim had done with his skywriting website, and so he owed her this, even if she insisted that he repay the favor on the holiday. And so he did, and no one got it, and then he was gone. Off to fly the four hundred miles home.

But there was someone there who did get it, or at least that's how it seemed to Amy. When Arnie had finished his maneuvers, this pale man in a tan linen suit stood up from his collapsible lawn chair, pointed at the sky, and mumbled something before he walked off. Amy was so sure he knew what it said that she tried to follow him, but there were a lot of families between her and him, and at one point she was encircled by a group of kids with lit sparklers, the youngest crying as she held a sparkler in each hand, unsure of what to do with them as they spit and shimmered colored flames and gave off a wild light. Amy wanted to help the poor kid, but her better instincts succumbed to her obsession with the message and with finding this man who might know what it meant.

When she saw him again he was eating two corn dogs by nibbling away at the fried cornbread and discarding the hot dogs and sticks. She couldn't imagine that even a vegetarian would do that, but it was what this man did, and because of his peculiar look and mannerisms, she suspected he might himself be some kind of alien visitor. Could they look like us? If so, then that probably meant we'd all been aliens too, dropped here from space and left to multiply until the ships might one day return. And they had returned. Amy had seen one, except they hadn't taken any of us back. Would she go? Maybe. Only if Jim went too, which was an impossibility, because he would continue to deny the existence of a saucer even as he flew inside one.

"Hey," Amy said to the man, who looked surprised that anyone would talk to him. "You knew what it said."

"Don't you?" he said. "You paid for it."

"I don't. I was hoping someone would. How did you?..."

"You're Amy Clinton. I'm the County Clerk. You had to register your event with us in order for us to approve the fly-over."

"But you know what it says?"

"It's the message in the sky," he said. "From your website. I Googled you after we got the forms. I had to make sure you weren't some kind of prankster."

"You don't think I'm a prankster?"

"You seem harmless. It's a kind of greeting. I don't know quite how it translates but you see something similar in a lot of languages. If you were to put this at the city limits, it would say enter and be welcomed."

"You look at that and you see 'welcome'?"

"It's a loopy hand but also direct. For example, the curvy lines suggest you are welcome while the crossed ones are more of a warning. You can come here, but only if you come in peace. It's what I pick up from basic handwriting analysis."

"And how did you recognize me?"

"More Googling. You came in third in a bake-off five years ago."

"The lemon twists. They could have been better."

"Third is nothing to shirk. Those other ladies looked hardcore."

"It was highly competitive and I haven't been back."

Amy looked past the fireworks in anticipation of seeing another glowing object in the sky, but none came. If they were there, they didn't reveal themselves. She wasn't entirely disappointed, because she suspected that she couldn't simply summon them whenever she wanted. But her hopes were up just the same. Jim had a great time, and she was sure the Trumps were there in the crowd somewhere, though even they probably wouldn't recognize what Arnie wrote. Then they went home, with a traffic jam to get out of the parking lot and another holiday over.

Jim Clinton woke up in a long hall with a fog machine and a spotlight behind him. He felt a low vibration aimed at his chest. The shadows of the little people who led him down the hall were disorienting. His handlers were disproportioned, with large hairless heads and big black eyes. They smelled of latex from their masks and the gloves that extended their fingers, but Jim didn't doubt their authenticity and he wouldn't remember these details that should have made him question the experience, even as it occurred.

He was brought to an aluminum examination table, told to take off his pajamas in plain English, and to sit on it, the metal cold on his butt and the back of his thighs.

"They can fly to Mars and back," he thought, "but they didn't think to keep the spaceship heated."

He was poked and prodded and all the while no one said anything, like the first guy who spoke had broken protocol and there wasn't going to be any more of that. Jim was dizzy and he wanted to get up. He decided he could go, that he could walk out.

The one closest to him stared into his eyes, the eyes like smoked glass. There were no whites and no eyelids, so the little guy never blinked.

Jim pushed him away with his foot and the being resisted but Jim easily knocked him over. He was done with needles and sensors for tonight, so he got off the table and walked back down the hall, toward the fog machine and the spotlight, which he passed and he saw he was walking on the ground. There was grass and trees and no spaceship but a series of black curtains hung around the area Jim walked out of.

He had just gotten his bearings when a soldier with a flashlight and a taser came over and said, "Where are you going? Get back in there."

He nearly replied, "I'm standing naked in the woods for some reason," but he was zapped before any words left his mouth, and when he awoke he had scattered memories he was ashamed to admit. So he buried any recollection deep in his psyche, only to bubble up occasionally when Amy insisted that whoever our visitors were, they had to be benevolent to be able to travel so many millions of miles.

hether one seeks answers to mysteries or shuts oneself off from possibilities, one topic leads to another and when Amy asked Arnie about chemtrails, he knew what that was. There was a Venn Diagram of belief hidden away at the Air Force and a similar memo at the CIA, where those who watched at night for UFOs, who went deep in the woods trekking Bigfoot, or who went out at dawn to scan the horizon for a glimpse of Nibiru—they also had a tendency to doubt the moon landing, to be skeptical of the official 9/11 narrative, and to take note of hazy skies seeded with chemtrails, which was to say that there was a widespread government program to use military and commercial airlines to spray the atmosphere with aerosols for an undisclosed reason. The theories for the motives behind such an activity ranged from shielding sunlight to help slow global warming, so the rich could milk every penny out of the oil reserves that were already paid for; to mask the appearance of Nibiru in our skies, so the rich could milk every penny out of global capitalism before the system crashed in universal panic; and/or to cover up the presence of UFOs in the night, so the rich could—no surprise—milk every penny out of the oil reserves that were already paid for. What do UFOs have to do with petro-dollars one might ask? It's not that aliens would prevent the burning of fossil fuels, though the practice is as primitive as cutting down a tree to make a fire to warm a hot dog. To be clear: the appearance of UFOs would not trigger suicides as a radio play about a UFO invasion once did, but if we took UFOs seriously we might come to understand how they worked. They required an enormous amount of energy in a small space, not by nuclear means, but something else, which could obviously power the planet with no carbon emissions, and that's what would defund oil and coal, and prevent wars for oil and coal, and divest the industries related to the production, transportation, and distribution of old oil technologies, as well as the industries that manufactured the wars of acquisition of these same resources.

So were they spraying the atmosphere with chemicals to slow the inevitable effects of such inefficient expenditures of energy, to allow for better radar imaging and to create a missile shield, to cover up the appearance of a rogue planet on the eve of another deluge, and/or to blot out the distant lights that traveled not like shooting stars, not like satellites, but like something else? Who is to say? There are those who can say but won't, those who do say but are ridiculed, and those who entertain the possibility but remain somewhere between those with the authority to know and those who suffer for opening their mouths unwisely. As time trudges, technology creeps, wars are waged, and money continues to pour into overflowing coffers. Some believe chemtrails create a reflective haze to project holograms onto, so when the time is ripe for martial law, there will be a fake UFO invasion like a movie in the clouds, or a fake second coming of Our Lord.

Amy Clinton didn't know for sure what any of this might mean, but she had read about it and the possibilities consumed her.

"What I was wondering," Amy said to Arnie Fishman, "was that if your skywriting is meant to stay in the sky and not dissipate, as a vapor is wont to do, then you might know something about these chemtrails?"

Arnie had also heard of this alleged phenomenon and was vaguely aware of the possible motives, without having spent too much mental energy as to the wheres and the hows. Did he believe our government would spray us all with something that would keep us complacent but also eager to go to work? Something that dampened our spiritual awakening while also keeping us going to church?

"I mostly work as a crop duster," Arnie said. "So I do know a thing or two about spraying noxious chemicals."

"What kinds of chemicals?"

"Round-Up mostly. If not entirely harmless it's at least legal. And in no way illicit."

"If I was sprayed with Round-Up would it make me hallucinate? Or if I saw an actual UFO would I forget? Or would I behave somehow differently?"

"No? Maybe? I don't know. You don't want it on you."

"Hypothetically, there could be a substance sprayed high above us that does something not revealed?"

"Yes."

"Like what?"

"I'm a bit of an expert in the application of chemicals and sprays, not so much in the uses and/or effects of said chemicals and sprays. Sorry."

"You're withholding."

"We're on the phone."

"Right. So if I was to meet you..."

"I don't know what else I might say. I'm 400 miles away."

"I'll ask Jim about encryption. He's more of a website guy but he's good at figuring stuff out. Then maybe we could email."

"So you're going to ask your husband about how we might email each other about chemtrails in such a way that the government won't know, yet we've already talked about it, here on an open line, and you have a UFO website, and you hired me to put a UFO message in the sky?"

"Nothing will happen. Do you think something will happen?"

"I just think we don't know about chemtrails or encryption or the government and why play with matches?"

"I think there are answers out there and we should be looking. I think we're of a like mind, Arnie, and I think you're more involved in this than you want to admit. Because you did write a message to the aliens and you didn't do it because of a website; you did it because you also believe."

Tommy Trump had lost weight. At first he didn't know how to be vegetarian. He thought it meant he had to eat vegetables, which were terrible for breakfast, were too often uncooked, and he never felt full. After a few days he realized it was okay to be hungry, and he acclimated. When they went to the same old restaurants he got strange looks from familiar wait staff for his orders. So they went to new restaurants and he discovered veggie burgers, fried tofu, and eggplant parmesan. He didn't leave the restaurant hungry, though he would be hungry later that night. And he always wanted to taste whatever Cher had gotten. She would suggest fish, but fish wasn't a vegetable.

"There are different kinds of vegetarians," she said. "Some eat fish. Some eat chicken. You could be one of those and you could still grill out."

"I could grill vegetables."

"Why?"

"Maybe they'd see me. And they'd know."

"You can't go around worrying about what people think."

"Amy thinks they wrote a message to us."

"To us?"

"To all of humanity."

"Who cares what Amy thinks?"

"Maybe they told us not to eat meat."

"Why would they?"

"The Bible tells people what not to eat. Maybe the Bible-people got that idea from a message in the sky."

"What if it was a scribe with shell fish allergies?" Cher said. "Or what if those rules came from a boy king who only ate Frosted Flakes?"

"I don't expect you to understand," Tommy said, "but I feel right about this."

"Okay," Cher said, "but if you ever email me a link to a PETA slaughterhouse video, we're getting a divorce."

"It's easier not to think about it," Tommy said. "But the videos are real and you know it."

"If it means not having to hunt, and not having to go hungry, then I'm fine with it," Cher said, "But you'll be back. You are thinking about a Big Mac right now."

"I am," Tommy said. "But I've learned to say 'no' and it's not hard."

"So what else did the UFO people tell you not to do?"

"No wars."

"You're sure?"

"No nukes."

"One of the letters does look like a mushroom cloud."

"No gods."

"There haven't been gods in a long time."

"We have gods," Tommy said. "They own things. They buy power."

"So no money?" Cher said.

"I think so."

"And how is that going to work?"

"It's not the money so much as the disparity and the division."

"I could get with that," Cher said, "But money flows up and it flows to those who control the spigot."

"No spigots then," Tommy said.

"They said all that? In those four squiggly letters?"

"I'm hearing it inside. In my soul. I'm open now and the universe has been let in."

"I like that," Cher said and she scooted close to him. "I mean I miss Tommy but I like the new you."

idicule and misinformation has been the single largest discourager of vegetarianism and of moving the planet in a conscious direction since humans have become more connected. There are religious institutions that preach vegetarianism but they tend to be isolated, in the way that entire cultures can be isolated from influencing the people who live elsewhere. Meanwhile dominant cultures have defined what counts as reason. Except that vegetarianism is reasonable. While mass production of living beings for the sake of consumption cannot be uncruel, it also devotes an unconscionable percentage of edible grains to these animals for the sake of the human palate. There's no more cheap arable land. Fresh water is becoming more scarce. If it weren't subsidized, we'd feel these pressures while buying groceries.

Now there are vegetarian restaurants and cookbooks with respectability, and celebrities who don't eat meat. Could a politician run with full disclosure of an ethical lifestyle with vegetarianism at the center? As much as a politician could admit that he'd seen flying saucers piloted by human-like creatures of vast technological ability and intelligence, and perhaps morals—at least that's how Tommy Trump saw them—smart, well-equipped, and good.

Was eating meat somehow evil or bad? Given where we are and what we know, despite the issue being obfuscated, possibly yes. If we assign responsibility to those who should not be ignorant, because they are smart about all kinds of other things, then probably yes.

A belief, which promotes a lifestyle, and which does not break laws, should be accepted. And where it encourages a greater good, it should not be discouraged. The pursuit of knowledge, and of truth, has long been considered noble. Yet those who publicly describe the things they've seen in the sky or the contact-events they've experienced are questioned as if they've lost touch, as if they're children, as if they don't know proper etiquette, that the truth is sometimes unspeakable, even if it might seem harmless. Yet, there were apparently harmless truths that were national security secrets. If, for example, there were UFO pilots in our air space that were not from our world, then that constituted an alien invasion and any information pertaining to these vehicles might well be classified and might also be tamped down by coercion.

Official-looking visitors from the bureau knock on the door and ask questions in such a way to suggest unhappy outcomes for answering the questions ever again. Such unhappy outcomes included but were not limited to: losing friends, losing a job, losing a lease or a mortgage, being taken forcefully for mental health evaluation, and/or the occurrence of accidental death or suspicious suicide.

Most had no idea they'd entered such an arena until they received the knock on the door. Many persisted due to their righteous determination until they'd ventured further toward the least desirable of possible outcomes. But sooner or later, even they got the message. And they may, after years, question what they'd seen. Or if they persisted to believe would only mention it in confidence to those they knew and loved, when the time felt right and there was a sense of close connection. Such moments are rare, such people extraordinary, and such connections special. Yet, the kinds of things that Jim, Amy, Tommy, and Cher saw on that day are not entirely uncommon and very good honest and sane people have seen such things for seventy-plus years, maybe thousands of years.

Some in power believe enough is enough, but they aren't highly placed or they'd know why the cat must remain in the bag while the rest of us don't see the harm in asking the obvious: if they are here, can't we at least say they are here; if they are here, who are they and what do they want; if they are here, did we do something to trigger their arrival? if they are here, what does that mean for our future? How should we approach them and how do we live afterwards?

It was only a matter of days before Amy Clinton had to tell Jim to turn off the comments on her website. He had used a template intended for blogging so each page had a comments section, and he had not thought to turn them off. It was easy enough, once she brought it to his attention, but he didn't have the time and could she let it go for a few more days? He had to tweak Arnie's skywriting website and he had to catch up with his coding for work. Since he was the coding guy there, and they had no concept of how long any particular task might take, he'd been able to occasionally fool them as he did no work for days. But with the two websites that he'd built and the days he took off after seeing the message in the sky, he had reached the limits of jacking around and he had to put in coding time for work. They'd met his wife and hadn't thought her particularly eccentric, but she was now, with her name on a shiny new website that he'd built, with an experience that was described that included extra-terrestrial flying machines where Jim Clinton was also a witness. Was Jim Clinton to be trusted as the company coder after that? I mean we expect our computer guy to be eccentric, but if he's trying to contact aliens is everyone okay with that?

rnie Fishman flew the yellow crop duster eighty-five miles to a field of Round-Up-Ready soy where he would make eight passes, then fly back to refill the tanks. The sky was turquoise and clear, but he had to admit he hadn't seen a haze-free ceiling in a long time, so there might be something to this chemtrail nonsense. He circled the farm to assess the best approach. At one end were power lines, at the other a row of trees along a dirt road. He made his first pass with a chemical cloud trailing the duster and he pulled up to twist the biplane around like a swimmer's flip-turn. As he descended for his second pass he saw three children in the dirt road watching him. He flew circles for fifteen minutes because they needed to move. The homeowner was warned about staying indoors. He'd dump the stuff on soy but that didn't mean he was okay with spraying these dumb kids. He couldn't call, he couldn't land, and he didn't have a way to signal, so he flew off. He kept the farm in view but went up to a higher altitude, just to look around. He'd give the kids half-an-hour, and if they were still out there, he'd charge the farmer and go home.

He watched a jumbo jet fly high above and he paid particular attention to the vapor trail. It didn't dissipate. And it didn't dissipate. And it still didn't dissipate. Then, moving along the path where the jet had been, an orb-shaped glowing red object caught up with the jet, flew circles around it, and sped off. As Arnie was still processing what he'd seen, two fighter jets pursued in the direction of the red orb. Arnie flew back to the farm, where, because of the fighter jets, he was sure those kids were never going back inside, but they were gone, which was puzzling. He couldn't imagine anything more exciting out here in the middle of nowhere than a pair of fighter jets, but the kids had left. So maybe reason had prevailed and the homeowner had called them inside.

Arnie flew low and he made his passes, but he had to be careful because he was distracted by what he'd seen. He kept playing back the image of the red orb in his mind. There was no doubt it was advanced and otherworldly. But why today? After all the years he'd flown, he hadn't seen anything like that. Was it because he'd opened himself up to the possibility, or was it that they were responding to the message he'd written in the sky? He *had* just written to them, to someone.

On his way back to refill with RoundUp, one of the fighter jets buzzed him and he wasn't sure but he got the impression there was something menacing about the encounter. He couldn't see the pilot but he could imagine him laughing. It bothered him all the way home, and when he landed he didn't really want to fly back. But a job was a job, and that farmer had paid for his RoundUp.

Jim Clinton stood at his laptop at the granite counter on the center island in the Trump's spacious kitchen. Cherise Trump sat on a tall bar stool next to him as he scrolled through website templates. She sipped on a glass of white wine with no idea what kind of website she wanted. Jim took swallows from his own glass though he was disinclined toward such a sweet wine and it was too early in the day for him to drink. But he didn't want to make Cher feel like a lush, and also this brainstorming session might take a while since Cher didn't have hobbies or interests, and they were having a hard time figuring out how she was supposed to present herself to the world.

"Something about animals?"

"No."

"Something about music?"

"No."

"A kind of open diary?"

"Probably not."

"A how-to?"

"How to what?"

"How to.... is there something you like to do?"

"I like baths."

"I don't think you'll get very far with baths."

"I like wine."

"There you go."

"But I don't really *know* wine."

"Right."

"Lets pick some colors maybe."

"Okay."

"What are some colors you like?"

"Maybe you could show me some."

"This is a color wheel. We can pick pretty much any color by moving the cursor around on here."

"I like that one."

"We can use this one. It's kind of a turquoise. Now what goes with it? Black maybe?"

"I don't want black."

"Just a little black?"

"No black."

"Purple?"

"No."

"A darker blue?"

"I don't want too much blue."

"Gray?"

"Gray is a lighter black, isn't it?"

"Not really."

"In a way."

"How about this: you move the cursor around and when you find colors you like, push down on the pad and that will save them."

"Like this?"

"Is that one you wanted?"

"No. I was just trying it."

"Wait until you find one you like."

"I like this yellow."

"It doesn't really go with turquoise though, does it?"

"I didn't know it had to go with turquoise. You said pick colors I like."

"You're right. I did say that. Pick colors you like and we can try to pair them later."

"I like this. This is fun."

"It is fun," Jim said. "Now maybe you could also think about what you want the subject of your website to be."

"I don't know."

Jim chugged down the rest of his wine and poured himself another glass. He stared at the gas grill in the middle of the kitchen island and he realized Jim could grill indoors. He didn't have to become a vegetarian. When he and Cher bought the house, the indoor grill that he never used was probably one of the selling points. Just as he knew it couldn't be easy to be married to Cher, he felt sorry for her because her husband was changed by the UFO encounter. Meanwhile, Jim knew himself so well that even if he believed the UFO was real, which he didn't, there was no way something like that would change him.

"Maybe we're beating around the bush?" Jim said.

Cher didn't know what he meant by that, but she was flattered because she supposed it meant he might want to sleep with her, which she hadn't expected because he was married to Amy. She scooched closer to him and ran a hand through his hair.

"Do you think we are?" she said.

"What I meant is that I think this is about what happened that day. You're trying to make sense of that day."

"I am," Cher said, but she wasn't thinking of the same day as Jim. The day she needed to make sense of was the one where Tommy was in the garden staring at Amy's tits while becoming a vegetarian.

"There's no reason you can't have a website about it. Your version would be different. You'd have different conclusions."

"Different than what?"

"Than the message in the sky."

"What are you talking about?"

"The UFO. The thing we saw. Whatever it was."

"Oh, I don't care about that," Cher said.

"Then what big day did *you* mean?"

Cher was embarrassed to realize they weren't having the same thought, and she sat up and leaned away from him.

"Amy is trying to steal Tommy," she said, and Jim wished he hadn't asked, because he was so surprised by her answer that he laughed. Cher was in the middle of some kind of marital crisis, and he outright laughed. Which made her turn bright red and he had to be careful because he'd seen her angry and he didn't want any part of that.

Jim held up his hands in a truce and he said, "Whatever you might think is happening, is probably not happening." He could explain to her that Amy was pretty much disgusted by Tommy most of the time, and the garden had really been his idea. Tommy wasn't in the best shape and wasn't even that good looking when he was. He had money but was mostly a prick about it, and there was no way Amy was going to see past all that and get naked with him. Instead, he said, "Me and Amy are pretty open with each other about everything and if there was something going on, even a little, I think she'd tell me."

"She'd *tell* you?"

"I know it sounds odd. But yes."

"Are you guys like swingers or something?"

"No."

"But like if you and I did it, which would *never* happen, you'd *tell* her?"

"I didn't say *I* would. But you're right. It would never happen."

"So *you* might fool around?"

"No, I wouldn't."

"Not even if she did?"

"Which she wouldn't."

"But if she did, and she *told* you?"

"I don't even know what we're talking about any more," Jim said. He had come over because Tommy was going to pay him enough to make this website for Cher that would make up for all the free work he did for Amy and the barnstormer, except it was turning out to be three times as much work and he may have also just entered into some kind of adultery pact with Cher. "Do you want to make your website about the UFO?"

"That's Amy's thing."

"If you think she's stealing Tommy, who is your thing, you can steal the UFO idea, which is her thing."

"You're right!" Cher said. "It would drive her fucking nuts! This is way better than sleeping with you."

"You were going to…?"

"Not now that I don't have to."

Jim drank half of his second glass of wine and he looked Cher up and down. He'd known her for so long and had never considered her in that way, though he did now, and he was surprised that he liked her. He really liked her. He never understood why she was with Tommy but everyone had someone and such pairings seldom made sense. Here he was, nearly in a pairing with her, like turquoise and yellow, that would have made no sense at all, but under the influence of wine, and with her admitting what she'd just admitted, he found he did want her in that way.

"You can have your own UFO website and it will drive Amy crazy, but there will be nothing she can say about it."

"Because I was there too."

"You were."

"And the best photos are *my* photos."

"They are."

"And I've *always* believed in UFOs. Not just in the past five weeks."

"I like it," Jim said. "We can start there," and he pulled up Cher's photo of the spaceship, which he had saved on his desktop, because he'd used it for Amy's website, and he'd made a cutout silhouette that he put on the pages as a kind of theme. He and Cher had been going nowhere for so long but he'd gotten to the core of what she wanted through her jealousy, and they were finally getting work done.

It occurred to Jim that this object looked nothing like what he'd witnessed during his abduction experiences, where he didn't remember seeing a ship at all. There were lab rooms and hallways, smoky forests and bright lights. Cher was cheerful in her belief in them and he didn't want to ruin that for her. Especially since she might tell Tommy, who was terrified enough as it was. Jim endured these kidnappings without really believing in them, so that he might be himself again the rest of the time. He knew that whatever was happening was momentary and he would wake up hung over, but otherwise right again.

Cher said, "I've always known something important would happen to me. And now I have a website to prove it."

Tommy Trump had a fear of them for most of his life. He was terrified by the *War of the Worlds* as a child, where they showed up to blast everyone for apparently no reason, and it was their mechanical representation, as ships, and probes, that made them so frightening. They were covered in protective shells and there was no reasoning with them. At the end of the film they were revealed as tentacled and monstrous. He supposed the radio play had the same effect, that it was their unknown natures more than their lethality that provoked fear. Thinking back on *War of the Worlds* gave him a kind of comfort, as he reacquainted himself with and nurtured a terror that had been with him for so long. The special effects were dated but impressive, though those representations had nothing on the reality of what he'd seen in the sky. The ship was larger, faster, and more powerful than any stop-motion animated model. As grotesque as the movie creatures were, there was nothing so unsettling as short fragile humanoids with bulging hairless heads and big black eyes. He hadn't seen them, but Tommy knew they were up there. If they wanted to communicate, the message couldn't be trusted, and it couldn't be good.

He didn't think praying would help. He didn't think any peace offering or military standoff had a chance. But then he remembered the end of War of the Worlds and how the aliens were accidentally defeated, by microbes and disease. And these little ones, the Grays, with their bloated bellies—hardly any muscle, and barely a mouth—they had to be susceptible. He remembered Steven Spielberg's *E.T.* sick and dying at the end and that's how he wanted them all. He would gladly move through the rest of his days with the flu or a cold, if it would keep them at bay. And he remembered how, back when he was going to church with Cher, they always passed that daycare with the "help wanted" sign in the window, with no better way of getting sick than to be around sniveling brats. So he asked Cher about Little Angels Daycare and how he might like to put in a few hours and this was more bizarre to her than when he decided to give up meat. Because when their own child, Tammy, was a baby, he couldn't be bothered to bottle feed her or change a diaper, and now, presumably because he thought UFOs were watching him, he was determined to be a better person?

"It's not called that anymore," Cher said. "It's Little Patriots."

"Why are they patriots?"

"Because they're not angels."

"And why aren't they angels?"

"Because one of them died."

"How are they still in business?"

"He didn't die while he was there. But when he died, the name was too much of a reminder for the parents from then on, because they went to the funeral, and the preacher had called him a little angel, and they put 'little angel' on his little headstone, and all of that was on the news. We watched it together and we thought it was so sad. But now they call it Little Patriots so everyone can get on with their lives."

"They're still hiring?"

"Every daycare everywhere is always hiring."

"I think I might like to help."

So Tommy went there and he explained that retirement had bored him, though he wasn't retired, and the first thing he wanted to do was to change diapers, which was weird and they wouldn't leave him alone with any of the kids without one of the girls observing him. So while they were happy to have the help, his being there didn't relieve the employee load, and they had to keep reminding him to wash his hands. There was even a time one of the girls said she saw him picking Kleenex out of the trash. Why would he do that? But then he'd call in sick and he'd be gone until he showed up again for a day or two, only to call in sick again, or to show up sick, which wasn't any good either, and so he was sent home. And he never seemed happier than when his nose was running or he had a cough. Sure, he looked tired, but he was cheerful, and so it really was good to have him around sometimes despite everything else.

Tommy had his favorites. He was partial to the girls, because he'd had one of his own and he knew how to play with them. They would own a restaurant and he would make a reservation to eat there. Or they would all be princesses and he was the knight who would kneel before them.

And if Tommy had his favorites there were also kids he didn't like, first among them a boy named Roger who he was sure was on the autism spectrum, because Roger went about childhood so businesslike, and he asked questions about things he shouldn't have known. Roger had never heard of soup. Roger couldn't understand what was so great about cartoons. And if Tommy was in Roger's presence for too long he seemed to see how the boy was too short, how his blonde hair was thinned, and how he sometimes looked like he had large black eyes. What Tommy liked least about him was the way Roger could tell any of the other kids what to do, even the princesses, and they would perform for him as unquestioningly and as sure as robots. Roger never got sick and he was also apprehensive around Tommy, who went out of his way to get sick, and so the man and the boy soon saw each other as adversaries, and Tommy had to be careful, because he was quite sure this strange boy had the means and the desire to get him fired. Tommy needed this job. The germs were his armor and he hadn't felt as safe since before the arrival of the UFO.

A trick of light in the twilight hours, the heat rising from an airfield bent the flashing apparition of an airliner as it approached for landing, or a lighthouse as seen from the mainland, or the chemically induced hallucinations from ergot fungi unknowingly consumed, or a sexual molestation papered over in memory as UFOs and aliens. Night terrors, drunk witnesses, and moonlight dispersed by fog.

One cannot discount the possibility of weather balloons. One can go a lifetime and never cross paths with a weather balloon, but they are here, they are odd, and they can sometimes look saucer-ish or otherworldly. As for E.T. pilots or Eben visitors, if one sees what one thinks is a spaceship, the mind can fill-in small humanoids. As unlikely as it might be, the appearance of a weather balloon could also happen on the same day as the accidental consumption of ergot fungi, or on a night with heat rising from an airfield. And a weather balloon may float low in the sky, at the horizon near Venus.

It's so easy to mistake Venus for a UFO that every college should require astronomy to discourage erroneous sightings. One might be surprised at how bright and flickering Venus can be. Drunks are especially easily baffled by the appearance of Venus. As for daytime sightings, Venus can show up in the mornings and evenings too, a bedeviling blue dot in the cerulean sky.

And so it goes: Venus, airliner, weather balloon. An unreliable witness and Venus, or an airliner on approach, or a lighthouse.

And let's not forget camera flare. Photos can produce artifacts from the camera that aren't being seen. We're mesmerized by a trick of light that's merely a byproduct of the lens.

And there's Photoshop. The deluded can spread any story, and create the images to prove it, some so earnest they believe their own lies.

Jim Clinton repeated these explanations to himself like a loop in his head, even when he was abducted, even when he was the unreliable witness and was ergot-ed out of his mind.

Parked in a dirt lot near the main entrance of the Elkhart County 4-H Fair, as families left for the night, Val waited for a fare hike on the Lyft Driver app. The Turtles concert was nearly over and "Happy Together" echoed across the neighboring fields. Val would wait until ten minutes after the final curtain before becoming an active driver on the app. Any longer than that and drivers would come from Goshen, which would lower the spiked rate and ruin her chance for a $20 or $30 ride.

Her white Toyota Solaris was covered in dust from the dirt lot. The engine idled and her air conditioner hummed. She drove out here, so she needed to get a good fare, and if the rates didn't shoot up soon, the night was a wash.

She watched the Enterprise ride, as it rose up, a fantastic disc covered in colored neon and bright white bulbs, the cars like shuttle pods with brake lights that streaked red as the ride achieved perpendicularity for a few revolutions before it slowly dropped back toward Earth. There were scant riders on the Ferris Wheel. They rocked the seats trying to flip all the way around. The Pirate Ship started up again and slowly built momentum as it swayed to higher peaks. She watched impatiently as the last riders spun and twirled and she thought about her bills. She hoped to make money ahead of the weekend with The Turtles concert.

Val drove for Lyft exclusively, but her friends called her Uber Mom, which she was, though it sounded condescending, except they liked saying it so much she never complained. She knew the sacrifices she'd have to make when she asked Drew for the divorce. She still loved him sometimes. He would go out of his way to extend a kindness, even now. She simply couldn't stay with someone who didn't believe her.

They came at night when he was asleep, so whatever she said didn't matter. When she sensed they were there and it was about to happen, Drew was always too deep in sleep, like he was drugged, and she couldn't scream, she couldn't run, she was never able to wake him. Drew was unable to protect her and when she told him about the incidents, he made her doubt herself. It was unfortunate that what she needed from him, he couldn't give, but what she couldn't abide was that he made it worse afterwards.

Drew was the one who suggested going to a psychologist, but his insurance didn't cover it, and the visits cost a lot. Val suspected that if she went to someone even tangentially related to Drew, then that person would make her feel crazy too. Simply going was a kind of admission that things weren't right. In time she discovered there were psychologists who believed. A lot of them were also trance mediums or they'd want to read her astrological chart, or to try to sell her vitamins, but some of them offered hypnotic regression and once she'd learned of it, Val was sure this was exactly what she needed. It wasn't entirely unscientific, but even if no one else believed her, they could record her session and she could listen to herself relate what she didn't remember. From then on she would know what had happened, and what would happen again. Because she moved but they found her. She drove all night on the days when her daughter, Kristen, was with Drew, because she didn't want to be alone at night. Though they could take her from her car and she'd wake up again, with hours missing, the Lyft app still on and pinging rides, her acceptance rate completely shot.

If she saved up enough money to go for more regression therapy she could verify, to herself at least, what she knew had been happening. Because she knew almost nothing about it. Except for her bills, which were undeniably real. When they took her while she was supposed to be driving she lost all of that income. And even when she drove out to the Elkhart County 4-H Fair after The Turtles concert and the fairgrounds were closing, there weren't enough riders to cause the rates to spike.

She accepted a ping twenty minutes after most of the cars had filed out, and her rider was a carny, a guy with greasy hair and a simple line tattoo of a raven on his forearm who said he ran the Scrambler and he wanted to go into town for beer and smokes, and could she also drive him back out here to his trailer? She could, though she knew by the time they got back there wouldn't be any more riders, and so she did all this for six or seven dollars and she'd have been better off staying in South Bend to shuttle the drunk college kids home from the bars.

As usual, she warmed to her rider once they got talking. He'd traveled around and worked nights in rural fairgrounds all over the Midwest and so she wanted to know, had he ever seen one, and he had. He said it was at a high altitude and he knew his stars and planets. This one didn't traverse the sky in a straight line like a satellite, but it curlicued.

"I watched it for a while," he said, "and I wasn't alone but I was unable to really point to it, or describe where it was, and then it was gone."

"Those things are real," Val said, and she said it with such conviction she didn't feel like she had to tell him any stories of her own, though she felt the hair standing on her arms as soon as she'd said it. She sensed that they were being watched, so she sped up, and shortly afterwards they were pursued by flashing lights. She felt stupid when she looked and saw her speed, which wasn't usually a problem out here, but who knew what a Goshen cop was going to do.

She slowed and pulled over and the cop drove up behind her. She rolled down her window then kept her hands firmly on the wheel until the cop walked up, her car bathed in otherworldly strobing blue lights that made her feel panicked, like when they came for her, and she wanted to tell the carny to run, though she knew not to, and so she waited as too much time passed, time always bendy in those moments.

"You've got a taillight out," the cop said, and Val's heart sank.

She had no idea what a taillight would cost or where to go to replace one, and if he gave her a ticket her night was not only wasted, but she'd end up in the negative.

"I didn't know," she said.

"I'm only going to give you a warning," he said. "But you've got to get it fixed."

She tried not to give away how afraid she was, but behind the cop in a row of corn there was movement and shadows, and she was sure she saw two of them, with their large black eyes, and she must have gasped, because the cop turned around to look and he saw a farmer running up the road.

"Officer!" the farmer said, "you've got to come quick! I've been vandalized. My crops are all knocked down and these kids are playing laser tag or something.

Val watched as a saucer lifted up from the field behind the two men and her fear solidified. She looked into the backseat and the carny saw it too. She was furious at her dumb luck of not having picked up a more credible rider, but she was glad he was there at least. Maybe his turns of fate and his lifestyle made him immune to their mind manipulations and he might be able to fight back. Maybe he would stick up for her, repel these aliens, and they could drive away.

This wasn't the first time crop circles had shown up in a field near where she'd been, but it was the first time she knew of that they'd been caught in the act.

"Did you see...?" she said to the carny.

And he responded nonchalantly with the last thing she would have wanted to hear: "There's one of them buggers right there."

Tommy Trump woke up hungry, afraid to walk down the dark hall to the kitchen, unsure of what he might eat. He stared at the ceiling as lights penetrated the curtain from the backyard and the bedroom brightened. He slid to the floor and crawled over to the window where he peeked out.

"Cher!" he said. "Wake up! Someone's out there!"

There were spotlights and directional speakers pointed at the Clinton's house and a man in an E.T. mask mulled around Tommy's garden. He was stepping everywhere, carelessly, and Tommy wanted to murder him.

He watched as his neighbor, Jim, was carried out on the shoulders of three men in identical masks. They were too tall to be aliens, Tommy knew that much. They lifted him into the back of a black van parked in the alley with its lights out. The one in the garden stood lookout. He watched to make sure Amy didn't come out and he turned around to observe the quiet neighborhood. Tommy ducked out of sight so he wasn't seen, and the man turned back around. As time passed the man bent down to check out Tommy's veggies. Tommy had had a fabulous hot pepper go missing and now he knew why. The man lifted his E.T. mask off of his face and he chewed on one of Tommy's cucumbers.

Tommy was furious. Whatever they were doing to Jim wasn't right, but to take that opportunity to steal from his garden was unconscionable. He knew exactly which cucumber the man was eating and it was nearly perfect. The cucumber only needed to ripen another couple of days and he was the one who should be enjoying it. He slid open the patio door and slipped outside. The man was so close that Tommy could walk up and strangle him. Except he didn't know who he was dealing with, so he crawled along the bushes and out to the alley where he went up to the back of the van. He pulled on the handle but the door was locked. There was movement in the van and he heard the muffled sobs of Jim Clinton, so he had to do something. There was no one in the driver's seat so he lifted a cinderblock and tossed it through the windshield, which caused the car alarm on the van to go off and the men in their masks came spilling out the back, but Tommy was gone. He ran around to the front of his house, used the key under the mat, and he watched out the kitchen window as they got Jim in his house as fast as they could before they sped off with no windshield.

Tommy made himself a fried egg sandwich on toast, which wasn't at all what he wanted to eat, but his garden had been pilfered, so he was out of fresh veggies until he went to the store.

In the morning he went out to the alley, where he saw pieces of windshield glass, and he went over to talk to Jim, who Amy said was still sleeping. Tommy told Amy she should be careful with her website. He said the government had noticed and they might come again in the night.

"What in the world are you talking about?" Amy said.

"Has Jim had nightmares about aliens?" Tommy said.

"Not that I know of," Amy said.

"Ask him," he said.

"He doesn't believe in them," she said.

"Ask him."

Tommy walked in on Cher as she meditated in the middle of their bed in her favorite yoga pants. There was something he'd wanted to ask her but he'd forgotten. He knew not to disturb her, out of politeness, but he wondered if it might also be dangerous to bring her out of it, like waking up a sleepwalker. Tommy had gotten better at meditating and sometimes he got pretty far out. So he knew it was best to ease slowly back into the material world. Tommy held his breath and remained perfectly still as Cher faced him with her eyes closed.

She said, "I know you're standing there."

"Can you see me with your third eye?"

"I heard you stomping around. You're like a quarter horse."

"I didn't know you were in here. I didn't know to be quiet."

"It's who you are," Cher said. "I accept you."

"I accept you too," Tommy said.

She opened her eyes. "Do you know what I'm asking the universe?"

"I'm supposed to guess?"

"I want answers."

"To life's mysteries?"

"I want to know why Amy's website gets more page views than mine. I want to know why she's obsessed with inkblots in the sky. And I want more coffee."

"I can get you coffee."

"More *kinds* of coffee. Like at Starbucks where they have something like ten thousand ways to make coffee."

"I think that's exaggerated."

"I'd be happy with fifty."

"Fifty kinds of coffee? Like flavors?"

"Flavors is only part of it."

"What else is part of it?"

"Iced or frappé or latte. Or some other way."

"You want an espresso machine?" Tommy said. "You're meditating because you want cappuccino?"

"I felt tired," Cher said. "Sitting with my eyes closed was making me tired."

"It's okay to nap," Tommy said. "You can lie down and nap."

"I don't want to nap," Cher said, and Tommy felt bad because he hadn't meant to, but he'd somehow made her upset. She wouldn't be able to meditate now and he wouldn't be able to make her fifty kinds of coffee. He wanted to walk away but felt he had to say something. Except he couldn't think of anything. At least not anything that wouldn't be upsetting, with Jim Clinton's fake abduction at the forefront of his mind.

"Inkblots tell us about ourselves," he said, finally.

"What?"

He hadn't managed to avoid upsetting her, but he'd started so he had to continue. "In psychology an inkblot is this thing that you project your inner-self onto."

"I know about inkblots, Tommy. I'm not stupid."

"I just thought maybe—since you called them inkblots—that that might be what they really were."

"So we've been visited by psychoanalysts? From space?"

"It sounds dumb if you say it like that."

The Major stood in Airman Riley's room, the Airman on his bed and meditating.

"What are you doing?" The Major said.

"Isn't it obvious?"

"You work for us. You only do it for us."

"I'm meditating. I need to keep the practice to be able to do it."

"You didn't go anywhere?"

"Indiana."

"What's in Indiana?"

"I like to go home."

At the office, Jim Clinton was amazed at how little they knew about what he did. The data sets were valid but the decimals had shifted. He explained that it would take several days for him to write a patch, but he knew exactly what was wrong and he could fix it in ten minutes. He didn't feel he'd cheated the company either, because he'd asked for several raises over the years, proving to them he was underpaid, and when they wouldn't budge he found ways to work less, and they also let him work from home a lot, which made not working easier. He and Amy made enough, though it was sometimes frustrating to see a clod like Tommy Trump and his trophy wife make so much more from what, he didn't know. He suspected Tommy had stocks, though he was sure that if he did Cher would always talk about them. So he thought there must have been an inheritance, maybe from Cher's parents, because Jim had met Tommy's parents and there was no air of money about them, rather the opposite.

After work, as Jim came into the house through the garage he was pleased with himself that the computer glitch at work had bought him a few days off, though he was still perplexed at getting less than Tommy Trump. Then as he walked into the living room to look for Amy, there on the coffee table staring back at him was the bust of a painted clay extra-terrestrial. It looked more human than the ones from his encounters, if that was possible, but it still had the black almond-shaped eyes, and it was smaller than us. For a moment, as his anxiety shot up, Jim had the unsupportable impression that this thing was real and staring back at him. He couldn't move closer and he felt his knees wobble as he nearly collapsed from fear.

"Amy!" he shouted. "Amy, what is this?"

She came up the hall from the bedroom and she said, "He's a Zeta! It's an original Christie Lewis! I got a really good deal!"

"What's a Christie Lewis?"

"She channels them and it inspires her sculptures. It gives you a scare, doesn't it? That's because it's authentic. This is what a Zeta looks like. I'm thinking of calling him Terry."

Once Jim understood what this sculpture was and how it had come to be, he sat down on the sofa to get a better look. The black eyes seemed to follow him and they stared as he leaned back and opened his mind to the possibility of these creatures piloting giant metal Frisbees.

"They're the ones who met with Eisenhower," Amy said. "They're peaceful and we had a treaty with them."

"Had?"

"We might still, but it's out of our control. When Eisenhower created MJ-12, he fell out of the loop and they operated without oversight. It's what he tried to warn us about with the 'military industrial complex' speech."

"Eisenhower was a good guy?"

"Total good guy. He also met with the Annunaki. He didn't like them and he told them to leave."

"Are you going to buy one of those too?"

"Maybe. Although they're not as interesting. They look like Greek gods, so whatever—the same as us with curly beards, and bigger and more muscular."

"Like Aquaman?"

"Kind of."

"Doesn't do it for you?"

"I want to get a Gray, a Plieadean, and a Mantid."

"We'll need a bigger coffee table."

"We'll find space."

"How much are they? We should wait until I get my bonus."

"What if Christie Lewis sells out? Then what?"

"She'll make more, won't she?"

"Not if they call her back and she leaves the planet."

"You think they'll do that?"

"They might. She has been on six interstellar voyages. That's why she channels so well and how she knows for sure what they look like."

"It does look real," Jim admitted.

"It's a way of bringing them into our lives and letting them know we're not afraid."

"Maybe we're afraid," Jim said.

"I'm not afraid."

"We don't know why they're here. We don't know what they want. There are stories of them doing experiments on us. And I'm starting to believe it. Can you imagine how traumatic that would be?"

"Those people are just not open to the experience. I would welcome an abduction."

"Don't say that, Amy. You don't know."

"This fella here," Amy said and she patted the Zeta on the head. "He gives me really good vibes."

"But he's not the only one," Jim said. "You said even Eisenhower was afraid of them."

"We won't get an Annunaki. But we need a Plieadean. And probably a tall white. And don't tell Cher. If she sees this, she'll want to buy all of them."

"Probably," Jim agreed. "But wouldn't it better if they were all over at their house?"

When Arnie Fishman got another email from Messageinthesky.net, he hoped it was for a second skywriting job, because as much as he liked his new website, it hadn't brought in any more business. Crop dusting was steady but seasonal and this new batch of young men either wasn't creative enough or solvent enough to propose to their girlfriends with skywriting.

The email from Amy was a personal one. She asked about Lindbergh. Apparently, on his famous flight he'd encountered spirits or gaseous sky-beings, or let's just call them what they were, space aliens, and they talked to him about flight. Was he delusional? Maybe. Was he sleep-deprived, disoriented, and hallucinating? Possibly. Did he believe that he had a close encounter where he communicated with sentient beings? Absolutely, he did. And did he talk about the incident as if it were real and important? Yes.

And what did Arnie Fishman think of all of this? Had he had anything unusual occur while he was in the clouds? What was his opinion of Lindbergh, as a fellow pilot, and as someone willing to stake his enormous reputation for the sake of saying something unlikely to be believed? Arnie hadn't heard any of this, so he went seeking on the Web and it turned out there were other famous men in planes who'd seen things they couldn't explain. Was it the thin air? Or had they made themselves more visible from space? Humans had finally accomplished the goal of flight, and if there were watchers, they'd certainly taken notice. Arnie had seen a glowing red orb pursued by fighter jets out in the middle of nowhere. This meant that what he saw had a radar signature and had gotten the attention of NORAD. It had a physical form. He didn't know how to tell Amy any of that and didn't feel comfortable typing his story into an email. If the military was involved he didn't know if he was allowed to talk about it.

Then another email from Amy came through. This one was more desperate and direct. She said a woman who was a big deal in the UFO community had seen her website when she bought some art from her, and she'd suggested that Amy go to this big UFO conference in Arkansas. Amy said she didn't know anything about conferences, but the woman told her it was easy. You wrote a proposal and if they liked what you planned to talk about, you were in. This was a really good one, with a lot of P.R. If they thought the speaker was a big draw, they sent a camera crew to have them make a teaser and they posted the videos to YouTube weeks before the conference, which the woman said would get thousands of views and it would insure a good audience when the conference rolled around.

She said for a first-timer it was better to submit as a panel. It would help her chance of being accepted if she knew others willing to talk. She couldn't see Jim being part of any panel, and she got the feeling Cher was angry at her for something and not about to let Tommy go, so she reached out to the skywriter, and sure enough, he did have a story. When he read Amy's second email, after some hesitation, he typed it all out, and suddenly the experience was more real. Yes, he could imagine going to Arkansas and telling a room full of believers what they already knew, that UFOs were real, and they could all work to uncover what the government was hiding.

He hit send, and Amy replied that it made her happy to know that there were strangers brought together by this who were about to embark on something very important. Then Arnie spent the rest of the week watching videos from the YouTube channel of the Arkansas conference, and one led to another, and he saw how there were personalities who made a living from the UFO subject, who projected a believability not easily discounted, and while for most of his life he hadn't given the subject much thought, Arnie wanted to meet these people, and to be one of them, to become someone who could speak the truth no matter how dangerous it might be, someone not afraid to gaze into the deep mysteries.

im had made it easy for Cher to use her website as a blog. She could log in, open the tab for the blog, give it a title, and type whatever was on her mind. She'd written about her experiences with meditation and the feeling that someone else was sometimes there. She'd written about her favorite yoga pants and how grateful she was for them, saying she didn't think she could meditate without them. She'd written that people can change: how one day a meat lover might become a vegetarian, or how someone you lived next to for years seemed cuter, and how you might imagine dating them. She wrote about how she'd always believed in UFOs but never thought she'd actually see one. And how she'd never owned a good camera but thought of herself as a naturally talented photographer. She could capture the moment and frame a good shot. When it had been a while since she'd blogged and she felt she had to write something, but didn't know what, she'd check Amy's website and see if Amy had put up anything new. Amy didn't have a blog but she might post a picture of a crop circle and give her thoughts about it. Or she might look for symbols like the ones they'd seen in the sky, to compare them to tattoos she'd seen, or ancient hieroglyphs. Amy's website was more visual, while Cher was more of a writer. And when she looked at Amy's website for the first time in a week, there had been a lot of activity. Amy had posted a link to a conference in Arkansas and she talked about going. She had posted pictures of alien busts displayed in her living room and said she would meet this artist at the conference. So all of a sudden it was like Amy *was* blogging, and Cher had thought of blogging as her thing.

Did this artist have any insight into who piloted the UFO in the sky that day? Amy was sure that if anyone knew—other than a government agent with above-top-secret clearance who was not likely to tell anyone, not even the president—then this artist who sculpted alien heads was a close second.

Cher went to the artist's website and while the sculpted alien heads were overpriced and kind of ugly, even primitive, Cher wanted several of them, mostly to post pictures of the heads in her own house and blog about them, which would drive Amy bonkers. So she made a wish list, and without hesitation she ordered herself a menagerie: an Andromedan, an Acturian, a Draco Reptilian, a Zuma Zeta, a Nephilim, an Insectoid, a Blue Avian, a Venusian, a Selurian, an Agarthan, a Nordic, a Melon Head, a Martian Monkey, a Sasquatch. They all arrived on the same day, stacked on her porch, so that she had a great unboxing. She set them around her living room, where they watched one another, suspicious of the motives of the other races. They were either ready to help humanity ascend or to manipulate us into another millennia of darkness. There was an ancient spiritual war represented in the Trump's living room and Cher photographed them and blogged about the attributes of each, as she understood them, sure to set off a spiritual war of her own, with her neighbor, Amy. And there inside one of the boxes was a note from the artist herself, who had addressed the letter to Amy, seeing the address on the same street in Nappanee and mistaking the order for another of Amy's, though the name on the order was clearly one Cherise Trump.

In her letter, the artist said she was glad Amy had found someone to order the items for her, so she had thought this order was Amy's and Cher was helping her keep it on the down low. In her experience, when a husband isn't open to the possibility of alien entities, the friction might make it difficult for Zeta to come through. She had done some channeling and had asked Zeta about the message in the sky, and Zeta told the artist it was the Tall Whites. Cher could have kicked herself because she hadn't bought a Tall White. She must have overlooked them as she was putting together her order.

In the letter, the artist warned Amy that her husband was having experiences that were real, but the abductors weren't extra-terrestrials. They were humans who wanted to do him harm. And Cher found herself in a dilemma. She couldn't bring up the sculptures until Amy had. She knew Amy stalked Cher's website at least as much as Cher visited hers, but maybe Amy would never say anything, upset that Cher had gone ahead and bought up a bunch of sculptures, which was Amy's thing as much as having a UFO website had also been Amy's thing. And now Cher was drawn into it even more, because Cher had accidentally received this personal correspondence from the artist that was intended for Amy.

Someone wanted to harm Jim, which was upsetting to Cher too, because she realized now that Jim really did like her that way, even if he said he didn't, and she felt protective of him now. If before she didn't want harm to come to him, just out of a neighborly goodwill kind of feeling, now she didn't because it might interfere with what fate had in store for them, Cher and Jim. And she realized Amy and the artist were going to meet up at this UFO conference, which was soon enough, and the artist could give Amy the info then. Cher also realized she was going to have to go to this conference, in order to smooth things over, and maybe this artist could also channel some answers for Cher, who, by the way, had spent a hell of a lot more on sculpture than Amy, and who had some questions of her own. Like who was the guy walking around in her meditations, also not an extra terrestrial. Was he one of the ones who wanted to hurt Jim, and was she indirectly responsible for attracting him to Jim. Or, like the artist, was Cher really good at meditation and also perceptive about the unseen?

Cher worried about Jim Clinton so much that she thought about him when she meditated. Sometimes she would set three or four of her alien busts around the bedroom to stare at her as she sat up in the middle of the bed and projected her inner-being outwards. She didn't want to commune with the aliens represented in the ring around her, but her intention was to commune with the Zetas, who were in touch with the maker of these clay personages. The Zetas had told the sculptor that someone wanted to harm Jim and she wanted to help Jim in a way that Amy couldn't. Cher wondered if Jim registering domain names for them was what made him a target, and she decided she could meditate a spiritual pushback against these unscrupulous anonymous government agents. This was her mood when her eyes snapped open and she stared directly into the painted eyes of the Blue Avian bust: she had the urge to go outside.

She looked out the front window where she suspected she might see an unmarked van, but there were no cars on the street, and the neighborhood was calm, except for a lone black man in a white Adidas sweat suit and gold Pumas who walked casually down the sidewalk. Cher couldn't remember the last time she'd seen a black person in their neighborhood and her mind was racing with suspicion just as her better self overturned each thought to be sure that she wasn't being racist.

Was it racist to remark on the fact that the man was black and also that there generally hadn't been any black people walking on their sidewalk? Was it racist to realize that maybe they'd gotten some new black neighbors and she hadn't even noticed? She was pretty sure that was the opposite of being racist, because a racist would notice right away. But then it probably was racist of her to assume he couldn't possibly be a new neighbor, which was how she felt, she didn't know why, except that he didn't fit in. He would have had to have walked a long way from where he might live, because she sort-of knew all the people who lived on the surrounding streets, if not by name, at least by what cars they drove, how many kids they had, and whether they were blond, redheaded, or brunette, because they were all white, which wasn't racist, it just was.

She wanted to ask him where he was going, or if he was lost, but she was sure that was racist. Still, she felt compelled to talk to him, especially if he was a government agent sent to do something terrible to Jim.

She made sure she had her cell phone and her house key and she went outside and pulled the door closed behind her so that it locked.

"Hey there," she said. "I'm Cherise. I was wondering where you got those yoga pants."

The man turned, confused. Realizing where he was, and after interpreting her meaning through the cultural confusion, he said, "I don't do yoga. These are warm-ups. They came from Costco."

Likewise, Cher had never seen a black man at Costco. She knew this wasn't her fault, but also knew that never in a million years should she say that out loud. And so she pretended that her astonishment was actually about the sweat pants. For her own part, she wore a favorite pair of expensive yoga pants that fit tightly and showed off her glutes, so that she stood to display her side silhouette. Obviously she wouldn't wear actual athletic pants of the looser variety, but she acted interested. She acted like she would.

"I've been looking for a pair just like that," she said, though it sounded contrived and she could barely make it through the sentiment without the moment collapsing in upon itself.

"I got them a while back," the man said. "They may have sold them all."

"Have you ever seen a UFO?" Cher blurted, and she immediately regretted it but couldn't take it back.

"Like space aliens?" he said. "They're not interested in us."

"Yes they are," Cher said, though she didn't know.

"We're all from somewhere," the man said. "None of us really belongs here."

"That is so true," Cher said, and she tried to go back into her house but understood as soon as she touched the doorknob that she'd locked it and she was going to have to take out her key to get back in.

"Accidentally locked the door," she said. "Luckily, I have the key," and she took it out of her pocket to show him.

He laughed and shook his head. Cher supposed this wasn't the first time a white person had accidentally locked a door around him. And she wanted to apologize and to also point out that it had nothing to do with him, but talking any more would make it worse. So she said, "See you around!" and she went back into her house where she collapsed onto the living room couch in embarrassment, though not too embarrassed that she didn't still lock the front door again before she lay down.

Surrounded by the rest of her alien clan, who stared at her and made her self-conscious, she wondered why there weren't any negroid alien races, or species, or if these alien species had races, and she suspected that if they'd been left out of the pantheon the sculptor might be racist, or maybe the Zetas she channeled were racist. She was so confused and upset, she didn't know what she believed. She'd been happy knowing there were all kinds of aliens, from distant planets, some who were like us, and some like Star Wars creatures, humanoid but also not. Now she doubted the reality of it all, and she suspected this sculptor was selling fantasies, maybe not intentionally, because maybe she deluded herself as well.

And so she pulled up the sculptor's website and she typed her an email, asking for a special request, a commissioned project. She didn't know how the sculptor would feel about it, but she had to have a black alien, or an African alien, or a Nubian, or whatever one might call them, because she'd gone out of her way to be inclusive, but was reminded of her oversight by a passerby in the neighborhood, and she wanted to know that he counted. If we all came from somewhere, like he said, then Cher wanted the sculptor to channel the Zetas and find out where that was. Even if it meant Cher was encouraging further delusions, she was okay with this. Because if Cher was delusional, at least she wasn't a racist.

Christie Lewis, in the middle of her California king memory foam mattress with bamboo-fiber sheets and a Himalayan goose down comforter, was having trouble channeling her Zeta, a being she called Freddie, who called himself Alfred, because she wanted things familiar, though not too jokey, so that she'd always avoided calling him Alf. Not really a him and not really a her, Freddie preferred the pronoun zeta, which wasn't really a pronoun, and was only distinguished from Zeta by dropping the capitalization. Freddie explained there were languages without pronouns, just as there were planets without air, and zeta wanted her to respect the differences, which might cause confusion, but only if she didn't ask the right questions, which was the nature of channeling, to send up questions on the long-distance telepathic line, with answers coming back true and direct, Freddie apparently unable to lie.

Because of a commissioned project that came from the neighbor of the woman Christie invited to the conference in Arkansas—she realized that now, that it was the neighbor who ordered all the busts—Christie wanted to know about black aliens, or African aliens, or Afrocentric aliens—she didn't know what to call them—were there aliens with racial features like black people? She seemed to remember that such a race existed, though, as always, she needed clarification and guidance from Freddie, who did not answer her inquiry, which was unlike zeta, and Christie took a deep cleansing breath. She tried not to project her frustration, and she reformulated her question, unsure of how to describe the faces of black people without emphasizing racial stereotypes.

After clearing her mind and sensing a connection with zeta, Christie said, "Why won't you answer? I want to sculpt the truth. That's more important to me than money. I want to get them right. Why won't you help me?"

And when she was met with silence, Christie did something she never did: she got up, went into the ceramics workshop and rolled out a lump of clay without guidance. She would work from intuition. She'd keep her connection to zeta open, and if no words came, she would listen for thoughts and gestures. She would glean zeta's meaning even if zeta refused to speak.

She pulled together the ends of the slab of clay to form a hollow conehead, then she rounded the crown because she wanted the species more human in appearance. She dipped chunks of clay in water and smeared them onto the face to build up features until she had a wide flat nose and large lips.

"Is this wrong?" she said. "Am I doing it wrong?"

With no answer she continued until she had the head of a hybrid, like the mug shot of an African-American male in his thirties, but with the large almond eyes of a Gray. She pressed amethyst crystals into his earlobes and at the third eye, to make impressions where she would glue them afterwards. Once she fired him in the kiln she'd mix black and bronze glazes to get a tint that wouldn't be right, but would be an earthy yet otherworldly metallic brown, and she knew she'd have to paint the lips red, which she understood as the problem and the reason for zeta's silence, because however practiced or well-intentioned Christie was with clay, she didn't have the talent to pull off anything but a pickaninny, and she couldn't put her name on it, or send it out as a representation of an extraterrestrial race, though she was close, and she wasn't ready to give up.

She rolled out a larger lump of clay, this time giving it shoulders, sumptuous breasts, a long braid of hair, the same almond eyes, and hoop earrings. This time she tried to make an African woman, pretty sure that unlike zeta, these humanoids were gendered, though what she'd made was worse. She didn't have to imagine the big red lips to understand the outrage her form would invoke. Freddie hadn't said anything but she felt like she was on the right track, and this second bust was as good as her Annunaki, or her sasquatch, except she didn't offend anyone if the alien features were exaggerated, yet her Africans always would. Freddie wasn't going to tell her if she was right or wrong, because this was as good as she was going to do, which wasn't good enough, and she was going to have to leave an absence in the gallery of galactic humans. Left with cartoonish depictions, she wasn't going to deliver them, because she didn't owe this woman anything, even if she'd bought up a good portion of her work, even if she might meet her in Arkansas.

Christie decided to fire the couple anyway, and to give them a glaze, though she was sure she was pursuing a disaster. She knew Freddie stayed silent because zeta couldn't lie, yet the truth was unutterable.

As Tommy Trump walked from the bedroom to the kitchen for his morning coffee, he paused in the living room where he was surrounded by the clay busts of aliens, and he was anxious that Cher had invited so many of them into their home. He understood the ones who looked like Greek gods—he couldn't remember what Cher had called them—who came to Earth thousands of B.C. ago because they wanted gold and women. They made lightning bolts and took whatever they wanted. He didn't like the way that one looked at him, a big muscular male with striking blue eyes. And he also felt the icy glare from the lizardy one. He couldn't remember what Cher called those either, but he remembered her saying of them, "Might is right," and so among the space visitors the scaly green ones and the godly ones were who Tommy best understood. He thought of them as colonizers and capitalists, and while he didn't exactly like being thought of as the colonized, he at least understood that he should be cautious of them. Because they would want to take his gold, and his woman. And from their point of view, their might would make that right.

He was relieved when Cher followed behind him from the bedroom, in her night robe, though he acted like the staring aliens meant nothing to him, like he hadn't been frozen here on his way to the kitchen.

"Coffee?" he said.

She walked past him, "Of course."

As they sat across from each other in the breakfast nook and the coffeemaker percolated, Tommy wanted to ask about the other ones, though he knew this would bring rebuke. "I've already told you about them," Cher would say. "Weren't you listening?"

He had been but he couldn't remember who among them were good, who might harm us, and who was indifferent.

"How do we know about them?" he had asked.

"Through contact, through channeling, through downloads."

"What's downloads?"

"When information is implanted in the mind all at once. One has knowledge one shouldn't. And the only explanation is that it came from them."

"The *only* explanation?"

"Can you think of another?"

"A really good guess?"

"We're talking about highly technical and specific knowledge," Cher had told him. "And these were experiencers."

"Abductees?"

"Some of them don't like to be called that. They see the experience as positive."

"Because of downloads?"

"That's one thing. Also, like, interstellar trips and stuff."

"Time travel?"

"Sometimes."

"It sounds like there's so much," Tommy had said. "How do you know what to believe?"

"You can believe all of it."

"Is that practical? Is that possible?"

"There's so much we don't know that's being revealed," Cher had said. "And I believe it."

"I do too," Tommy had said, but he had no idea what he was signing up for, except that there might be muscular invaders who wanted his money and his girl. This made sense to him. Of course they did. But time travel? How in the hell were they going to do that?

As they sat across from each other in the breakfast nook, Tommy remembered the look of the antagonistic aliens in the other room and he was sorry that he couldn't protect Cher from them. If they could manipulate his thoughts. If they had laser beams and antigravity spacesuits. If they had true knowledge of the past and future, then what could he do to keep them from taking her? He thought maybe they could get a dog. A big dog. He remembered back when they were dating and they told each other stories about their lives growing up, she had told him her family had had a husky named Tip. He shivered when he imagined a dog with ice-blue eyes the same as the Greek-god aliens, but he knew he could love a dog, and so this seemed like a good idea.

"What kind of dog would you want," he asked her as he set his coffee down and reached for her hand, "if we were to get a puppy?"

"You want a puppy?" she said and she brightened, more than when he told her Jim Clinton had agreed to make her a website. "Really?"

"I think so," he said, but he knew so. With a dog around he might be able to believe everything. And the scary ones might not be as scary. And the friendly ones, if they were truly friendly, would probably be happy to greet a dog too.

ecause he supposed the Major had cameras on him, and that he probably had enlisted men on the payroll who watched him, and maybe even other remote viewers who looked for him as he went outside himself, Airman Riley learned to remote view while doing other things. He'd gotten good at stepping out of himself as he played poker, and he had a regular game on Tuesday nights in the rec room, with a movie in the background while everyone drank canned beer. He would lose hand after hand, so he'd only bring what he was comfortable losing, and he wouldn't remember anything anyone would say, but this was a way for him to go out on his own, and to find the answers he needed. Because if the United States Air Force was going to use him for national security, he had a right to know why.

Tonight, as he sat on a pair of sevens, and the penny bets escalated, he walked into Amy and Jim's house, where he saw the clay sculpture head of a Zeta, and he knew he was on to something.

Amy was on the phone and she said, "Yes, yes. I understand."

She spoke with Timon Bowland, the assistant director of the Ozark conference, and he said he was inclined to accept her proposal on Christie Lewis's recommendation, but since Amy was new to the UFO community, since she didn't have name recognition, it would be better if she would submit with a panel.

ᛗ

Christie had told her as much, but Amy thought she'd try anyway because if she was going to put a panel together she knew Jim wouldn't go, and she might get Tommy to go, but then would Tommy try to pay for everything, and would he get up in front of all those experienced UFO researchers and talk about vegetarianism? And would he bring Cher? And if he didn't bring Cher would there be sexual tension, because there'd be limited space and they might have to share a room. But she'd need a third for a proper panel, and of course Cher would come, one more thing Cher copied from Amy, and she'd have to get Jim to come anyway because if Cher came that meant Tommy and Cher would share a room and there was no way she was going to be a third wheel the whole weekend. She wanted Jim there with her, to make the reservations, and to pay for things, and to do what a husband was supposed to do. Because whether he believed in what they'd seen that day or not, he was still her husband and he was going. She'd also mentioned the conference to Arnie Fishman, and he seemed to want to go.

"Can I do this over the phone?" Amy said.

Timon said, "I don't see why not. Let me get an application and I'll fill it out for you."

So Amy gave Timon Tommy and Cher's names, and Jim's too. A four-person panel of eyewitnesses of the message in the sky, with Arnie as an alternate, just to be sure. But when Timon heard that Arnie was a pilot he said he could get his own slot. He could still be on her panel, but pilots had instant credibility. So it was settled and Timon accepted her application over the phone, pending the conference fee, which he was also willing to finalize, if she had her credit card ready.

Airman Riley learned the names of these experiencers and he knew where they would be the week of the Ozark conference. He even memorized Amy's credit card number. Because he'd done it before, he followed the signal to the cell phone tower and bounced around until he was in Timon Bowland's office with a long list of experiencers of no use to anyone but himself, because the C.I.A, F.B.I, N.S.A, Naval Intelligence, N.O.R.A.D. and N.A.S.A, all surely knew about everyone going to the Ozark conference, most of whom had been before. In fact, it was a right of passage to anyone participating in a UFO conference to be visited by the men in black, who were sometimes men from the C.I.A, F.B.I, N.S.A, Naval Intelligence, N.O.R.A.D and N.A.S.A, though sometimes not, and Timon told her this. They'll show up to intimidate but fade away after the conference.

There wasn't any talk at any conference that was going to go letting cats out of bags because the good intel was always mixed with planted intel, equally as crazy, and who would ever be able to distinguish between them, especially when the speakers on the professional UFO circuit repeated nearly everything passed along to them. They needed to appear to be in the know to get paid appearances, unlike Tommy and

Cher, and Amy and Jim, who knew almost nothing about what was really going on, though they'd gotten a glimpse that day. But knowing everything and not being able to distinguish the facts from the lies was just as bad. Because this Amy person was new on the scene, Airman Riley knew this made them interesting to the C.I.A, F.B.I, N.S.A, Naval Intelligence, N.O.R.A.D. and N.A.S.A, and he decided he would try to do what he could to protect them. But Timon sensed him in the room. He looked right at Airman Riley, and Timon said, "I think you should leave."

So Airman Riley returned to his poker game, where he'd run out of pennies and the movie still played. He said he needed to pack it in and he left the game to go sleep until noon.

Amy had committed herself and her neighbors to the conference in Arkansas, but she hadn't gotten around to inviting them. She called Tommy and asked if she could have one of his peppers, since she knew he had plenty, because she'd picked out all the varieties, and he told her to meet him in the garden. Amy went to the front of their house to let herself through the gate, and soon she and Tommy were bent over to peek under leaves as Cher sat lotus-style on the bed in the bedroom with the curtains open to watch them.

"Has Cher had any luck with her website?" Amy said.

"What kind of luck?"

"Has anyone contacted her?"

"No, what's supposed to happen?" Tommy wanted to know. He'd been a vegetarian for months now, and no longer afraid to go outside.

"We got invited to a conference!"

"We?"

"They contacted me, but we're all experiencers. We all saw it."

"What kind of conference?"

"Only the premiere UFO conference in the nation."

"They have UFO conferences?"

"Of course they do."

"Are you going?"

"We should all go."

"What would we do?"

"You've been to conferences. What does anybody do? We show the pictures and we talk about it."

"People would listen?"

"It's the right audience," Amy said. "They would believe us."

"Jim's going?"

"I haven't told him. I think he would go if you all went. Cher would get to meet Christie Lewis."

"Who?"

"The artist. The alien sculptor."

"That's the last thing we need. We don't have any more display space. And Cher's got it in her head she wants a black one."

"A black what?"

"A black alien. Do you want me to talk to Jim?"

"No need," Amy said. "He'll go if I promise hotel sex."

"How much?" Tommy said. "If you don't mind me asking."

"I'll start at once-a-day, he'll push for oral, we'll closeout with something like a lukewarm honeymoon, but then we'll both be too tired to follow through. All told, we'll probably have sex twice, maybe three times over four days, the same as if we'd stayed home and I was getting him to clean the bathrooms, do the laundry, and take out the trash."

"We have a maid."

"I know you do."

"And we still have sex."

"I know."

"Cher has been working out and wearing these yoga pants."

"..."

"But you know that."

"I know that."

"Don't turn around," Tommy said. "She's watching us through the window. She thinks we flirt and it makes her jealous."

"That's so ridiculous."

"Ridiculous as it may seem, if you bend over I may get it twice tonight."

"You're using me?" Amy said.

"I'll talk to Cher about this conference," Tommy said. "And we'll all go. Is that what you want?"

"I really want to go."

"Then we can all get what we want. It's kind of beautiful, isn't it?"

Naked and sitting on a cold aluminum table, Jim Clinton was alone with a tall extraterrestrial. Jim listened as the being spoke English, in Jim's head. At least that's how it seemed, because the words were muffled and the mouth of the alien didn't move. The creature pointed to a star map on a screen on the wall with long fingers that didn't bend, where Jim was told they came from, and he also came from. He was one of them, and if he'd ever felt like he didn't belong here, now he knew why. He was a star child, a visitor carried by his mother like the Virgin Mary, and they were here to disclose his origins. He had dormant powers but must keep quiet and patiently wait. The Earth was being laid to waste and when the time came they'd arrive to take him, to return home, where he'd finally be with his people and at peace.

Jim had so many questions. Like why didn't he look like an alien?

Because there were alien races who looked human.

And how could he be something he didn't believe existed?

Because he was left to fend for himself, to blend in, to draw the wrong conclusions if need be, but he knew who he was now. He had to. If he searched himself he'd see.

But why now, if the laying to waste of the Earth was still some decades off?

So he could prepare. And so he would take the website down. He needed to keep quiet or the government would be on to him.

The government?

The government.

Couldn't his people protect him? Or could they take him back sooner?

The website's got to come down.

But it's not mine. And Cherise has one too.

Who?

The lady next door. It was mostly her photos.

Oh, that's not good.

They're nice people.

If the government comes they can cause a lot of pain.

You know, now that I think about it, I don't remember ever seeing the outside of this saucer.

You saw it.

I can't tell you what it looks like.

You're overwhelmed.

Can we go outside and look? It's important to me. It would help me understand.

Not right now. We're focused on the website.

Websites.

What's the other one called?

Cher's Reflections.

No wonder it eluded us. It's not a very good name for a UFO website, is it?

It's a blog. If you're so advanced, why can't *you* take them down?

It's better if you do it. If the provider gets complaints about hacking there could be a trail that leads them to us.

Your UFO has an IP address?

Sort of. It's technical.

Try me, Jim said. Tech is my thing.

Sometimes we have to do things the old-fashioned way.

All right. If it's important to the clandestine nature of whatever you're doing. But then you've got to leave us alone.

We will.

And I can't take anything down right away.

Why not?

There's this conference coming up. I'll need to leave them up for at least that long.

Oh, no no no. That's no good.

It's non-negotiable. I don't care who you are. There's hotel sex that's been promised, and I'm not missing that for some alien brothers who wait all my life to finally show up—because I still don't believe you.

We can get you sex.

Hotel sex. With my wife. It's very important to me.

Will you take money?

After the conference, I'll see what I can do, but until then you'll need to kindly fuck off.

Jim hadn't told Amy, which felt like a betrayal, but he had to talk to a professional. He was sure he was cracking up. He refused to believe he was visited by aliens, except he had concrete memories. So he booked an appointment, where he almost left the waiting room before his name was called, because Dr. Z was running late, but then a woman came out of his office, and she came out crying. Jim supposed Dr. Z had given her time to compose herself, and that was why they ran late, but he also had a schedule to keep, and here she was. When Jim saw her, he felt a longing. She needed help and he wanted to help her. With no words exchanged, he'd ponder the mystery of her suffering until he met her again, the same time the following week, when he still didn't dare talk to her, but he observed her more closely.

He pegged her as a single mom, who worked too hard and was frayed. He could see that if these abductions continued he might wind up like her. He wanted to know what tragedy lived in the pit of her gut. He wasn't sexually attracted to her, but he wanted to date her. He wanted to know what Dr. Z knew about her and he wanted to make it okay. He hoped she hadn't lost a child. He knew some things were unfixable, and he hated that maybe something unfixable plagued this woman.

Jim Clinton knew enough about depression to understand there wasn't always a cause, that it could fester for no reason at all. Jim had been depressed when the UFO showed up, and it gave him the idea that they had always been there, they had always taken him and done things to him, but he was only able to recognize the abductions now, because he'd been made aware by the message in the sky. So even if Jim understood depression might arrive without notable cause, in his case the cause came later, and it revealed itself as having silently undermined him all along.

"I'm so sorry," he said to the crying woman, who wasn't crying this time, though he couldn't shake that impression of her.

"Don't be sorry," she said. "The regression therapy returns you to those emotions. I want to know. I have to know. It's better for me than keeping it all inside."

Once Dr. Z understood her financial situation was a direct result of her abductions, that she worked as a Lyft driver and hadn't had steady employment for some time, he could no longer charge her for what she really needed.

And there was Dr. Z waving Jim into his office, so his conversation with Valery was cut short. Jim had so many questions. He wanted to stay there in the waiting room to talk to her. But he was there to see Dr. Z and he couldn't delay any longer.

Once Jim was seated in the recliner, Dr. Z asked about a regression again, if he wanted to try. He hadn't wanted to before, but now he did. Jim needed to know, though he had retained the memories. At least this way he could get an outside opinion.

Dr. Z did his thing by making subtle suggestions. He circled the recliner, he rubbed his fingers together near Jim's ears, and he eased Jim back in the recliner until Jim was in a trance. Jim talked and talked. As he did, he listened to himself, aware that he was the one talking, and the one listening. When he listened to himself like this, he understood that the aliens were really human people dressed as aliens, that they tortured him to scare him into keeping quiet, and they always incapacitated him with some weird drug.

Dr. Z also came to this conclusion, since Jim was explicit in his descriptions of the experiences. Dr. Z burned a DVD with a video of his session, and Jim watched it and thought about it when he got home. His problems weren't from the abductions themselves, but because people manipulated him into believing they were from space, which he didn't believe but also did believe, so there was trouble in his psychic core.

At night, when Amy was asleep, he would sometimes watch the session with Dr. Z, and he knew for sure what he'd always known, that his UFO abductions were a farce. He watched himself in the recliner as he addressed his tormentors, "Why won't you leave me alone?"

He said it to Dr. Z on his next visit, and Dr. Z agreed, but Dr. Z said something Jim hadn't expected, just as unsettling: that the reason Dr. Z knew Jim's abductors weren't extra-terrestrial was because he'd given hundreds of regressions to people who really were taken onto spaceships. Because the stories they told were all the same. The same emotionless distance came from the captors, the same routine procedures ad nauseam, and the same strange errors, like putting their clothes back on inside out, or dropping them back off at the wrong spot. Dr. Z didn't say it, but Jim knew his other patients, like Val, were real abductees. It made her grief tangible and something he could understand, since he'd had similar experiences, though counterfeit, while hers were authentic, and accompanied with just as much shame.

Part 11

Two F-18s were in pursuit of a cube-shaped craft that moved in quick jerky bursts like a computer cursor and not at all like an aircraft, since it was not aerodynamic, had no front or back or bottom, and didn't appear to have any kind of propulsion system. Yet, here it was, above the Ozarks, in advance of the nineteenth annual International UFO Symposium, as if it were a hired publicity stunt, and those who'd arrived early would have bragging rights, while those who came later would marvel at the video footage.

When he learned of the conference, Airman Riley recessed into his mind and he went deep to walk around. The spaces he could go included the conference hall, the hotels, and the digital realm. He saw lists of attendees and their email correspondence.

He saw credit card transactions with flights and rooms booked. He saw the conference brochure.

There were lectures and presentations that promised unseen footage of the many identifiable kinds of UFOs, and footage of the UFO pilots. Airman Riley knew how the titles of the talks would be seen with skepticism anywhere else—with subjects like implants, hybrid babies, and gravity propulsion systems that would be laughed at anywhere else—but Riley'd been around the unseen universe and he knew things, and he knew the hominids were real. And yet, there were talks he was excited about sitting in on. He'd been inside a saucer, had even piloted one, but he knew little about the six-fingered inhabitants, and there were scholars who would go to Arkansas and have an audience open to discussing everything. If his situation were different, he supposed he could stand at a podium with a laser pointer and tell them what he knew too. Although remote viewing, which was all the rage six or seven years ago, had become passé, and it was possible, despite his abilities and his impressive resumé, that if he'd sent an application to the conference, he might have had his proposal rejected.

He wanted to hear about sacred geometry, about Tesla's notebooks, and creatures of the fourth dimension. About the similarities between the frequencies of distant stars and whale songs, about element 115, and the hollow moon, and the hollow South Pole, and a model of the universe that had us careening behind the sun, pulled through a viscous substance with Earth trapped in the vacuum made by the path of the sun. For all that his unique advantages had shown him, there was so much Airman Riley didn't know, and he wondered how he would've concluded anything about anything if he hadn't been able to walk around in it. These were people who were mocked as unreasonable and unserious, yet so sure of what they believed that he wanted to hear them talk. He hoped the Major wouldn't impinge too much on his time for the next few days, because he was already going to have difficulty choosing among competing sessions, and Riley couldn't stand the thought of the Major pacing and peppering him with questions as he tried to listen and also lie about where he'd been. Lying was never good for his karma, even lying to someone as duplicitous as the Major, because Riley's abilities depended on a life of good conscious choices. How could he seek the truth and lie about it at the same time? He needed a vacation and more than anything, he wanted to sit in the audience, in the flesh, to be able to ask questions, to buy cheap paperbacks from fringe presses, and to be able to shake the hands of those who had devoted themselves to the hidden and the unknown.

So when the Major came pacing, Airman Riley decided he had nothing to lose. He told him what he wanted, and he asked very politely if he could go.

Of course they could get him the alias and the credentials to get in.

"But other agencies will be there watching," The Major said, "and we don't want to tip our hand."

"Aren't we all on the same team?" Riley asked.

"Not if we know what they don't know. It puts us in a better budgetary position."

"For black projects?"

"Not black."

"Unacknowledged?"

"Calling them that is a form of acknowledgement."

"Am I a black project?"

"You are a very important line-item with a title that sounds nothing at all like what you do."

"A blank check?"

"If the success of your activities relies on anything that costs money we can get it."

"I can go to this conference just by closing my eyes," Riley said, "but I want to be there. I want to wear a badge, drink gin and tonics, and sleep in a hotel bed."

"If you're trying to get laid, we can provide that."

"It's the first I've heard."

"If that's the underlying issue."

"We don't know what this might do for the project. I'm asking if I can go."

And instead of thinking it over or finding better ways to say 'no,' the Major gave in.

"Okay," he said, "but we're sending someone with you."

"A babysitter? A handler? You're like the KGB."

The Fish Analogy

Which goes something like this: that like fish we know nothing about what occurs beyond the surface, since a fish who looks up sees a mirror reflecting back, or if the fish sees anything on the other side of where the water meets the air, the fish sees abstract images without context or meaning. A fish is easily caught with nets and lures, and if the fish spends more than a terrified minute on a boat, and is able to escape back into waters, and to somehow communicate what was seen, would the fish be believed, and if believed would the tale last more than a generation? This is the conundrum we find ourselves in: a great disbelieving and a great forgetting, the situation of this fish not unlike the humans in Plato's Cave, unable to distinguish between what is seen from what is real, and unable to know a reality beyond what is seen that may be even more real. And we, who stare at TV screens and play video games and Photoshop ourselves to share with others who Photoshop themselves, know this as well as Plato or any fish. There is the 3D physical world, or what can be described and predicted by the earliest of modern physics, Newtonian mechanics—pre-relativity, pre-quantum mechanics, pre-multi-dimensional string theory—described as speed equals distance over time, in simple yet sometimes quite complex terms, the normal versus the paranormal, with no room for the weird, and magic is reduced to tricks with sleight of hand, hidden chambers, and smoke and mirrors. UFOs and ghosts, UFOs and E.S.P, UFOs and demonology—all inhabit the same Dewey decimal—though our modern world is moving quickly into realms with invisible architectures, with parallel universes, and knowledge secreted away by handshake societies, where opening a door may lead to another, further into the disbelieved and the forgotten, to be ridiculed by the cave-wall watchers and the great school of fish, never questioning from whence the shadows came or what lies above the surface of the water. Because here we are, inhabiting a thin skin of atmosphere with little insight into what is beyond, though there are those of us who have seen them, or dreamed of them, or been spirited away by them, only to return to have to try to make sense of our fishy lives, where the ceiling of sky won't let us see out, where our past is obscured by politics, and our connections to each other are fleeting or artificial. How much can we know? Quite a lot, if specialized and compartmentalized, with so much to read, and so many conferences to attend, including conferences on UFOs, where we can ponder the great mysteries without ridicule, for at least three days in the Ozarks, where we are encouraged to believe and our questioning and our knowledge-making is without limits. Though there are government agents, and they can listen in on our phones, and there are Christian protestors who believe, like some of us also believe, that the UFO agenda is soulless and ungodly, so that seeking out star visitors is akin to summoning demons, and we will soon regret this collective inquiry. One was here recently, chased away by F-18s like angels, for the kingdom and the power and the glory.

In the lobby of the Best Western Inn of the Ozarks, the presenters wore business dress while everyone else tended toward the regalia of Comic Con attendees, with minted Marvel/DC t-shirts of extra-terrestrials like The Guardians of the Galaxy or The Silver Surfer, bright yellow, green, or purple dye jobs, or full latex masks of both sinister and benevolent Grays, charm bracelets with various saucers, rockets, and comets, and accessories like cellphone cases decorated with star charts, the periodic table of elements, or a partially decimated row of Space Invaders.

In plaid shorts and a mint blouse, though she looked summery, if not festive, Amy Clinton felt underdressed. She'd gone out to Dunkin' Donuts to get a coffee and while she was glad she had it, she also wished she hadn't made the stop. Because when she got back, Cher was sitting with Christie Lewis on the front porch of the hotel, with all the lounges taken. Cher wore a lavender skirt suit that had probably cost a couple thousand dollars, and she wore too much gold jewelry, but she knew how to sit, her back straight and with her rump the only part of her that touched the chair, so that her suit stayed pressed, her hands crossed and rested on her knee as she leaned toward Christie who was in her element, here amongst her people.

Amy knew, because she followed Christie's blog obsessively, that Christie had a table in the main hall where she had busts to sell and she was debuting some new species, which Amy had already convinced herself she could do without for at least a year or two, when eventually the price would come down. When Cher saw Amy, she waved her over. And when Amy stood in front of the seated women, Cher introduced Amy as her neighbor and a fellow experiencer. Which made Amy's head nearly explode, because if she hadn't bought some of the sculptures herself and posted the pictures to her website, Cher never would have heard of Christie Lewis. And to Amy's surprise, Cher also explained that she'd bought several pieces herself, which made Amy even angrier. Did she have to say it like that, "several?" Because it meant Cher had bought more than Amy, maybe even a lot more, and she wanted Amy to know.

Amy leaned over to shake Christie's hand, and Christie lit up with recognition when Cher said, "You wrote to us about Amy's husband. You told us the Zetas had said it had been humans abducting him and he needed to be careful."

"Wait, what?" Amy said. "*My* husband?"

Christie nodded.

Cher leaned so far forward that only the slightest portion of her rump made contact with the chair and she was exhibiting some impressive core strength to be able to sit like that.

Amy said to Cher, "What do you mean 'wrote to us'?" She couldn't believe something so horrible had been happening to Jim and Cher knew but hadn't said anything.

"He blocks it all out," Christie said. "But someone from the government wants Jim to believe that aliens are real."

"They are real," Amy said.

Christie said, "They want him to think aliens are here to hurt us."

Cher had seen some of the less-friendly sculptures in Christie's menagerie and she scooched back in her chair. "Are they?" she asked.

"They each have their reasons for being here," Christie said. "Some are rooting for us. Some are not. A few think we deserve what we're doing to ourselves."

"But *humans* are abducting Jim?" Amy said. "That's kidnapping!"

"Some people have that authority," Christie explained, "and they justify it with 'national security'."

"Please don't tell Tommy," Cher said to Amy. She couldn't stand the thought of him reverting to the terror he'd experienced in the days and weeks after they'd seen the message in the sky, when he was afraid to go outside and he had to change himself fundamentally before he was okay with the idea of alien pilots above Indiana.

"He already knows," Christie said. "He intervened on Jim's behalf."

Cher felt warm inside. Because if there were aliens here to harm us, Tommy had guns and Tommy was a good shot.

Christie said, "His intervention was a turning point and the abductions have ceased for the time being."

Cher was awed by how much Christie knew about their little corner of Indiana. She'd only just met her and it was a testament to the power of her connection with the Zetas. Her insights confirmed the authority of her art. Remembering this emboldened Cher to ask about the status of her commissioned project.

"Have you asked them about the African aliens?" Cher said, which caused Christie to slump back in her chair, and for Cher to also slump back.

"They've been quiet on this," Christie said, "and it's not like them. It has never happened to me."

"What's this?" Amy wanted to know, because not only had Cher tried to hog Christie Lewis by buying lots of busts, but apparently she'd commissioned one.

"Well, I was thinking," Cher said, and she sat straighter, delighted with herself, "that we see lots of *species* of E.T.s, but we never see *races*."

"Except on Star Trek," Christie said, "and I happen to know that Roddenberry was talking to the Zetas too."

"I wanted to buy an African," Cher said, and as soon as Amy understood that such a race existed, she wanted one too.

"Why won't they help you?" Amy said.

"My hunch," Christie said, "is that it has to do with *representation*. I don't think I have the artfulness to accurately and respectfully represent them."

"What does that say about your other pieces?" Cher said, worried that all the aliens she'd bought could be suddenly devalued by such an admission.

"Race is tricky," Christie said. "We can be honest, well-intentioned, and try really hard to get it right... and yet, still come out looking really wrong."

"He doesn't have to be perfect," Cher said. "I want one."

"I haven't given up," Christie said, "but right now it seems like I may have to refund your money."

"Maybe there's a key to making an African?" Cher said. "Maybe you'll hit upon it."

"Maybe I'm not the right person for the task."

"But the Zetas know these Africans?"

"They haven't said."

"Is it possible the Zetas are racist?"

"Anything is possible, but I don't think so. It's more likely that we are, and that's where I'm blocked."

"You think *you're* racist?" Amy said.

"Isn't everyone a little bit?" Christie said, and while they agreed with this idea in principle, they rejected the notion that someone as enlightened as Christie Lewis could be racist. She had the help of the Zetas after all, which to some put her on a footing with the Buddha, Jesus, and Nostradamus.

"*You're* not," Amy said. "I might be, but you're not."

"*You're* not either," Cher said to Amy. "Not in a million years."

"I might be," Christie admitted, "and the Zetas might be too."

The extra-terrestrials were not the whole story. There were subterranean aliens and aliens underwater. With the vast expanse of space, a natural template for the imagination—all one has to do is look up—yet, there's so much unknown about what's below: ant people and reptilians in tunneled cities and fortresses, or our own nuclear-powered underground bases, justified by continuity of government and supplied with decades of canned food and bottled air, man-made caves where the wealthy go to survive, because of the red A-bomb button, or a meteor, or Planet X, a known / unknown calamity, and we saw it coming / we didn't see it coming, manipulated by TV and separated from our natures, never sleeping under the stars, but always knowing the thin layer of moist air on the only planet known to support life was fragile, and vulnerable, and if the mighty dinosaurs couldn't last, why would we? Digging in the garden unearths creepy-crawlies, digging deeper we discover the fossils of other epochs, and digging deeper what hell or hollow might be uncovered?

The space traveller is clean in puffy, white suits, while the dirt diver is smeared with the dust of ages. Below are dragons. Below are cave bears. Below is a refuge we enter at risk, with hearth-heat and pressure, with incubating grubs and dormant epidemics, where the hopes of unconventional dreamers take root as the optimists stare up. Better to let them come out when they're ready than to go seeking and to disturb them. Better to wait, though their arrival from the depths will herald something awful. Maybe the ant people will take a few of us down again to wait it out and survive. Maybe they listen to God, or to the Star Council and the meek shall inherit. Or maybe they're angry because of what we've spoiled, their Earth too. Where the rockets go, it is cold and quiet. Down below are resonant tones and drum rolls, heartbeats and mucus flows. Are we more afraid of the attic or of the basement?

The bar of the Best Western was renamed The Interstellar Lounge for the duration of the conference, when it would go back to being The Broken Spoke. There was a drink called The Vulcan mind meld that everyone had to try once before reverting to the old standbys: beer, vodka soda, or gin and tonic. The Interstellar Lounge was a place where experiencers and astrophysicists could sit together, where hypnotists and ancient alien historians could swap stories, and where incognito government agents listened in. There were a few favorites on the jukebox that got played over and over: Neil Young's "After the Gold Rush," Styx's "Come Sail Away," and anything by Boston, the songs accented by the sharp collision of billiard balls, the pool table the domain of a few players who came with their own cues and who mostly played each other. Some of the patrons could remember when the Interstellar Lounge wasn't crowded, and when cigarette smoke hung in the air, the bar having been smoke-free for years, with a huddle of smokers outside the front entrance and the occasional conference attendee bumming one and luxuriating in a feeling they hadn't allowed themselves in decades.

Because of their day jobs, there were UFO enthusiasts who had to sometimes travel to cities for regular work-related conferences, where the drinking was harder, the smoking less nostalgic, and the women had to fend off unwelcome conversations as politely as possible until they finally communicated their disinterest in blunt idioms. At those conferences, where the company picked up the tab and the talk was abstracted by buying and selling, they tried to enjoy themselves as much as possible, but the drinking was tiresome, while here, at the Ozark Conference, it elevated them, as they pontificated about their favorite subjects: our unknown origin, our place in the pantheon, and our return to our peaceful, soulful natures. At work conferences these men and women felt out of place, considered themselves geeks among wolves, and they often sat alone. Yet, here, everyone was weird and there was hardly a table with a solo drinker. One who sat alone was a robotics guy who was sketching out schematics after an eureka moment, another was a quiet Hoosier in an Air Force t-shirt. He knew he should have worn something else but he hated shopping and the t-shirt made it easier for him to be obtuse about himself without lying. He supposed they'd think he was a government agent anyway, so why not wear the t-shirt, which an agent wouldn't do, and Airman Riley found himself alone at his table, his rum and Coke flat and the ice melted, his eyes closed as his awareness wandered through the hotel, the walls and doors permeable to his spirit, with no idea what he was looking for until he saw it, and it saw him.

In room 332, accompanied by a human companion who was a deaf bespectacled light-skinned African, there was an alien with a tall afro who wore iridescent rainbow knee-high platform boots, a mostly unbuttoned disco satin shirt, and a gold pyramid amulet on a gold chain necklace. Here they were, African and Afro-Alien, and while the first was disinclined to leave his companion alone, the second was too self-evident to leave the room, especially here where everyone was on the lookout for aliens among us.

Airman Riley was hesitant to go walking about while his body sat in the bar, but he'd gotten bored and he wasn't sure but he thought he detected the aftertaste of NutraSweet in his rum and Coke, though he hadn't ordered a diet. So he didn't feel like drinking, didn't feel like sending it back, and while Springsteen's "Pink Cadillac" played in the bar, he'd gone walking about, with no particular agenda, and he'd come across the most interesting pair he'd ever encountered. He knew, because of his hyperawareness, that the visitor's companion was deaf, but that they could all talk telepathically, and he was soon engaged in a conversation of the close encounters kind. Because he suspected as much, Airman Riley opened with, "Are you from Venus?"

To which the tall alien replied, "You know it, my man."

139

"And how was the trip?"

"Smooth."

"Why are you here?"

"It's a party."

"Do you have a message?" Airman Riley said. "Is there something you want me to tell them?"

"The ones here, or the ones back there?" the alien said, which Riley understood as the ones at the conference, the believers and dreamers; or the ones back at the base, like the Major and his superiors, who intended to use his gift for tactical advantage.

"They have ways of knowing," Riley said, "and so they may ask me about you. What should I tell them?"

"It's the Age of Aquarius. Get a suntan. Build the love bomb."

"They won't hear that."

The deaf man interjected the telepathic conversation at this point, and the voice Airman Riley heard was educated and eloquent. He said, "what you do, then, is simply add to the end of any of these suggestions... 'or die'."

"Get a suntan, or die? Build the love bomb, or die?"

"It's all figurative anyway."

"These guys are anti-poets," Riley said. "They believe in what they do, and they believe it's good. They have very little imaginative capacity beyond the literal."

"'Or die' can be taken literally."

"It's going to motivate them the wrong way. It's how they operate already."

"We can't help you, then."

"But we need help."

"Obviously."

"Brotherman," the alien said. "You're talking to the wrong folks."

"Get on the docket," his companion said.

"I will," Riley said, and he realized that if he acted without regard to consequences, everything was easier.

To the extent that music exists in the mind, it maintains hope as a form of interspecies communication, while sound waves, that cannot traverse the vacuum of space, have less utility. Light, which can be converted from electromagnetic waves to sound waves also suggests this same hope, though less so. While we understand that the speed of light is very very fast, given the vast expanses of space, it's just not fast enough. Minds can be connected, instantly, across space, and so consciousness, the recognizer of communication, while not the antenna, may be the key to listening: us listening to them and them listening to us. We need shelter, we need rain, we need a cure for disease—are you listening? We need relief from tyrants, we need what money keeps from us, we need true understanding—can you hear us?

Venturing out into the town of Ozark Springs one understands why the site had hosted so many weirdos for so long—remote enough for the eccentric to take refuge. Tolerance comes in the quieter form of ignoring thy neighbor or recognizing that one can be any old way while the safest, most traditional, and structured lives have the benefit of community institutions, paychecks, and not having one's name whispered around by one's neighbors. Which isn't to say that they don't like having a UFO convention for one weekend every year, or that they don't themselves sometimes attend lectures on the analogy of the fish, or to hear tales of molemen and underground aliens. Many locals also believe, simply by the odds, because with all the other galaxies and planets why would we be the only ones? While they might reject such a notion outright as unbiblical, despite the Nephilim, and Jacob's ladder, and Ezekial's wheel. Most locals approach the likelihood as, "Anything's possible, I just don't believe in it."

The gas stations sell deep-fried burritos and fried chicken on a stick. There's an abundance of baseball hats, but none with the logos of baseball teams, and there's no baseball being played, except by the peewees, who soon grow out of it once they inhabit larger bodies. There are lusted-after girls aware of the power of their attraction, and young women, too young, but already pregnant and soon overweight and kept in kitchens or at the reception desks of dentists and government offices. The doctors here have been transplanted from other cities, other cultures really, the Northern metros, or the nearly Northern metros of Atlanta, Austin, or Raleigh-Durham. The restaurants are also imported, of the same fast-food varieties, though one can also get a burger at the bowling alley or at one of the seven bars.

When pilots speak people listen. These are men with military backgrounds. They have scientific minds. They employ an exactitude that allows them to lift into the air and land safely, time and again. They have nothing to gain by telling stories. In fact, they can be blackballed. And there are hundreds of pilots in the air at any given location, all the time. They fly above the clouds and can see for miles. If there is anything up there, a pilot would have a better chance of seeing. A pilot estimates velocity and a pilot is aware of our current state of technology, even if most of the basic mechanics of jet flight are nearing one hundred years old. Are there secret military programs with craft built on newer propulsion systems? Those vehicles would require pilots, and even military pilots can't keep secrets forever. With so many other pilots in the air, the experimental flying machines would be seen. But would they be recognized for what they were, or would they be termed "out of this world"? A pilot is more likely to proceed cautiously before drawing conclusions, and a pilot might recognize gravitational thrust, portals, or cloaked invisibility.

Without knowing this, but sensing it, Arnie was surprised at the number of attendees seated in the hall as he stepped to the podium. His background gave him an authority that Amy, Cher, Jim, and Tommy just didn't project. They had the pictures and they could corroborate their story, but he had an audience that was really listening. This was something he'd never experienced before. He could tell a family to stay inside if he was crop dusting and they may or may not follow his instructions. But here, at the Ozarks Conference, he was believed and his worldview was accepted as true.

He began by showing slides of a plane performing barnstorming maneuvers, and he led into shots that he took from the plane as he approached then flew through his barn. It was a dramatic series of photos, but had he been at some barnstorming conference they would not have had the same effect. Here, he was seen, not just as a pilot, but as a pilot of considerable daring and skill.

He explained that he was hired by Amy to duplicate the message in the sky and he showed the photos for comparison. He'd never made letters quite like them, and he described the technical details of the sky dance that produced his facsimile. He was proud of the result, especially when he told them that he encountered a UFO within days of this job, which he believed to be a correlation. He could see this last bit of information turning in the minds of his audience and blossoming into delight as he told them he planned to repeat the maneuver later that afternoon over the Best Western.

His final slides were of the ship he'd encountered, and while he didn't have any photos of the UFO, this was an audience used to seeing sketches.

"I'm not much of an artist," Arnie said, "but you get the idea."

It was smaller than the craft Amy and Jim saw, and it glowed red. For those who had missed the show in the skies in the days preceding the conference, Arnie had all but promised another. And for those who came, and who believed, but had never seen one, this was almost too much.

He got the feeling that maybe his talk wasn't as successful by the end as when he started. But then a hand slowly went up to ask where and at what time he would be skywriting, which he was sure he'd already said, but several of them wrote it down, or put it in the schedules on their phones, and he hoped, for their sakes, that something really would happen.

At the end of a long day at the Ozark Conference, with her head spinning from so much new information—subterranean aliens, pyramid builders, Antarctic bases, Majestic 12—but mostly, Cher was wondering how Christie Lewis, perhaps the most enlightened mind-traveller Cher had ever met, could think of herself as racist. It was absurd. And because she'd developed a habit, she'd missed meditating during this long day, but she finally got her chance while Tommy used up all the hot water in the shower.

She sat in the middle of the hotel bed in her lavender skirt suit, without even changing into one of the several pairs of yoga pants she'd brought along, and with her eyes closed, she soon found herself walking through the walls of the Best Western, from room to room, without too much embarrassment about imposing on the privacy of others, because none of them saw her. Until one of them did.

He sat in his room at a table where there was some kind of large electronic device and he listened in with clamshell headphones as he took notes. When Cher came through his wall, he stared straight at her. She came to the unsettling conclusion that this spy was somehow connected to the ones who were doing what they were doing to Jim, and she wondered if there coming here had brought him, or if they had somehow implanted the idea of coming here into Jim's mind, and he was the one who suggested it to Amy. Either way, there was someone at the hotel spying on everyone and he now knew that Cher was aware of what he looked like and what he was doing. He also knew that Cher had special psychic abilities. This traveling around, as unexpected as it was when Cher first started doing it, was also what she had imagined the end result of meditation was supposed to be, so she hadn't told anyone, because it had seemed unremarkable. But now she understood that it was quite remarkable, and she didn't know how to bring it up, because she was sure it was something that would make Amy insanely jealous. As much as Amy liked to believe that she knew more than Cher about meditation, there was no way Amy had been doing this, because there would have been blog post after blog post on Amy's website about her psychic travels.

Cher stood staring at this unfriendly man, unsure of what to say or what to do, when another man came through the wall. In shorts and an Air Force t-shirt, he led her away.

"He's harmless if you ignore him," the man said. "It's best not to draw attention to yourself."

"I've seen you before," Cher said. "I thought it was a dream."

"It's like dreaming," Airman Riley said, assuming rightly that Cher was a novice at out-of-body experiences, and he took her up onto the roof of the Best Western, a flat roof with an uneven tar coating, loud air-conditioning units in a row along the far side, and scattered trash from the last crew of roofers to come up here. There were stars shining through thin clouds and noise from a party in one of the rooms, where the sliding door to the room was open and smokers were out on the balcony.

"You can go anywhere," the man said, and he looked up to indicate the stars, "as long as you remember where you are and you don't stay too long or forget to come back."

"How long is too long?"

"When you feel a loosening, like the string that stretches back to the body has unraveled and the wind that blows is all that's left."

"It sounds scary."

"Not if you remain alert. Now where do you want to go?"

"To talk to the Zetas."

"I don't know who that is."

"You've never heard of the Zetas? It's where they're from."

"But I don't know where that is," Riley said.

"Did you go to any of the talks?"

"I must have missed that one."

"I'm feeling the wind," Cher said. "Like you said."

"You should go back."

"That wasn't very long."

"You'll get better at it."

"You think I will?" Cher said. She'd never had a mentor before and she liked the feeling of someone coaching her.

"I'm sure of it."

A program like SETI, the Search for Extra-Terrestrial Intelligence, that has been active for decades, can be defunded, with the researchers sent scrambling for private backing. But what kind of return on capital can come from that? A historian who writes about Nikolai Tesla will have his books relegated to an independent publisher and an editor with a poor sense of design, the yellow lettering on the cover of the paperback in a font that's blown up beyond its intended dimensions, a book to be ordered directly from the publisher's website and not in any libraries. A physicist who has demonstrated negative entropy and has pulled energy out of a zero-point system will be warned off the project by friends and colleagues or fired if she persists, the contents of her garage seized, and no engineering job applications sent afterwards to ever result in interviews.

One can talk about UFOs, because they can be explained away. One can post photographs of aliens, because the more real they are the less real they look. One can posit the extra-terrestrial origins of our species, and re-imagine Jehovah as some star traveller. One can even suggest that UFOs have crashed and some of our most significant technological advances came from reverse-engineering the components aboard these craft. But once one inquired about how the craft was powered, or how it travelled at such distances and accelerated so rapidly that it would kill any occupant, then this is knowledge that is considered off limits. If our energy systems are still theoretically about as primitive as cooking a hot dog over a fire, that's because most of the money flows have been built and maintained around such unsophisticated energy dispersals. Even a nuclear reactor is a version of cooking a hot dog over a fire. And an electric car? Charging the battery required the equivalent of cooking a hot dog over a fire. So that our energy systems are inefficient and outdated, but what else could there be? What else, indeed, and any UFO researcher has good guesses about where the inquiry might lead, except that UFO researchers are ridiculed, their ideas cheapened with misinformation, exaggeration, fakes, and outright denials. The smart ones won't talk about what would transform modern society into a new age of equality and prosperity, because the prospect of unlimited free energy, as liberating and uplifting as it would be, also comes with a fear of terrorism or cataclysmic revenge from people who can suddenly unleash energy weapons as easily as starting up the electric car, and no general worth their stars will ever allow that. Persistent and naïve scientists who can't take a hint can be harassed like Jim Clinton, or even disappeared in the name of national security.

But Jim was no scientist. He was pretty good at computers but didn't even believe in aliens, despite having witnessed a UFO. So there were other topics that couldn't be talked about, and the one Jim, Amy, Cher, and Tommy had stumbled onto was a direct communication. It's not that the message proved the existence of intelligent otherworldlies, as fantastic a discovery as that would be, but the fear, from those at the top, was that if avenues were opened, then the free-energy solutions would be disclosed. So it was a different way of ending up in the same place. A physicist might go about solving the world's problems by re-imagining the devices that utilize the flow of electrons, and Jim might encounter a being who decided Jim would really benefit from that kind of information. Do E.T.s have compassion for us, and would they help us like that? We really don't know, but what gets prevented in the name of national security are those kinds of possibilities, because once the secret is out, there's no going back, and more importantly, there's no good way to profit from free energy.

A brown sedan with government plates stopped at the ticket gate of the Ozark National Forest and one of the dark-haired agents got out to walk around the booth as the other chatted with the park employee.

"It's eleven dollars for the day," she explained.

"But we're here on government business," the one behind the wheel said. "I have a badge."

"No one said anything to me about that," the woman in the booth said, and she didn't know who to call. She hoped they would just pay, because at the end of the day there would be a car out there without a pass and she didn't want to lose her job.

"If a police car came through here, lights a-blaring, you wouldn't stop them and ask for eleven dollars, would you?"

"You don't have those kinds of lights."

"But we are police, we are on duty, and what we're here for is important."

The second agent, after having circled the ticket booth four times, stopped to ask, "Does this thing have an outlet? Are there other outlets?"

"I've got one in here," she said. "They told me there was a guy who brought a small TV, but ever since the antennas went digital, I don't know how that works. There's no wifi and I'm not about to pay a data overage to stream. Sometimes I plug in a fan."

"How do you keep occupied," the agent who stood too close to her at the window said, "without a TV?"

The woman understood she was being made fun of and she didn't appreciate it. Whatever it was these guys wanted, she didn't have to give it to them. If they thought they could insult her and also boss her around, they'd gotten the wrong impression.

"How would we find outlets in the park?"

"There are RV hook-ups in two of the campgrounds, but other than that, it's primitive sites."

"Do the RV campgrounds stay busy?"

"Of course. You'd need a reservation. Usually months in advance."

"And we couldn't just borrow an outlet out there?"

"Whoever had paid to use it probably wouldn't like that."

"If we needed in here at night," the driver said, "how late are the gates open?"

"There's a parking lot for hikers that stays open. They still have to pay admission, but they can come and go in their cars without the gate being locked. That's on the west side."

"So there's no booth?"

"There's a booth, but the gate stays open."

"And this booth has an outlet?"

"I don't know. Same as mine, probably."

"You ever seen anything weird out here?"

"Weird how?"

"Spooky lights. Campers sky watching on clear nights. Missing time."

"We get some weird people. Nature-types and hippie-types. I suppose they look at the stars. I don't get much chance to talk to them."

"Anyone else ever talk about anything strange, the rangers or anyone?"

"I sit here. I take eleven dollars. I swipe a debit card or I make change. I give them a receipt and a ticket. I tell them to display the ticket on their dash, and that's about it. Sometimes people wave at me when they leave. Sometimes I tell them no bottles and no beer, but I don't ever leave this booth to check."

"What if we told you people have seen UFOs?"

"You haven't ever seen anything like that?"

"Is this about that conference?" she said. "Most of them don't come out here. You should go talk to them. I'm sure they could tell you things."

"We were already at the conference."

"We thought we might come out here. Where people are more down-to-earth."

"You can say that again."

"But you've got nothing for us?" And the agent walked over to the passenger side and got back in the car.

"Some people say D.B. Cooper came through here when he was on the run," she said.

"I've never heard that."

"They say the same about Derringer, though, so it's probably an updated version of some old tale."

"There's truth in some of these fictions."

"What is that supposed to mean?"

"We may come back," the driver said. "In the mean time, ask around. See what people are saying."

And while it had never crossed her mind too often before, the ticket agent was spooked. They had reminded her how secluded the park was, how there were weirdos, and how there might also be good spots for UFOs to land unnoticed. She got the feeling that scaring her was what the two men had wanted to do, and she waved as they drove off.

"Thanks a fucking lot, guys."

While she refused to let them win, her eyes would dart at any movement in the distance under the dark canopy, and she was permanently unsettled. She had considered herself lucky not to have to work at Walmart, but now she was rethinking it. There wasn't ever no "missing time" at no Walmart.

Val posed a question to the Lyft Drivers Facebook Group about the road trip she planned to take. If she left early enough she could pick up riders on her way across Indiana, but what she also wanted to know, was if she would be able to drive in other states? Val's mom agreed to watch Kristen for up to two weeks whenever Drew couldn't. If things worked out—if she was frugal and slept in the Solaris every night—she could actually come away from the Ozark Conference with a small profit. Her route would stay in Indiana heading south, and would cross into Missouri through Southern Illinois, avoiding Kentucky, where she wouldn't be able to drive it turned out, because of something different about the registration process. This was mostly rural America, where demand would be down, but the distances were longer, so if she picked up the occasional rider here and there, she might make enough to cover her gas and meals. When she was in the cities—West Lafayette, Indianapolis, St. Louis, Memphis, Little Rock—she was guaranteed fares. Her progress would be slower, but she'd always have money that she could cash out from the Lyft app.

Dr. Z wanted her at Ozark, asked if she would be comfortable talking about her experiences, and hinted that coming forward might make her abductors back off. Because whatever else we might know about them, which wasn't a lot, we knew for sure that they went out of their way to keep their activities secret: they abducted at night, they flew in invisible ships, they suppressed memories. As she drove, Val rehearsed her story, from when she was a girl being lifted up in a beam of light in what seemed a game, to being taken as an adult, with a marriage ruined and a daughter she wanted more than anything to protect from them, though she was helpless to do anything. And that was the worst of it, not so much what they had done to her, which she was learning to remember through regression therapy, but that they would also very likely do these things to Kristen too. If she had left instructions with her mother not to leave Kristen alone, it wouldn't matter. Saying anything would only make her sound crazy and it might attract them, since they seemed to thrive on her fear. With her mother's memory also suppressed and her mother as helpless as any other human, what was the point? Her mother hadn't stopped them when they came for Val as a girl. Dr. Z suggested getting a large dog, and she would have, except only small dogs were allowed on her lease, and she didn't want to have to pay the pet deposit. As it was, she was glad every time she picked up a new passenger, because she hated being alone, and if the anxiety came over her when she was with someone, she could make small talk to try to tamp it down. Sometimes this worked, but afterwards she became depressed that there were so many people on the planet and hardly any of them were aware that we were being watched and could be plucked from our lives, tagged, and monitored for future abduction.

Outside Indianapolis, she picked up a Phoebe who took three phone calls from people she would meet up with later, and Val wished her own life had been so simple. It wasn't that she couldn't have friends, or that if she disappeared one night she couldn't come up with a story to cover her exit, but she'd have lies to keep track of, and it was just too much. Being honest was never an option. She'd learned that much from Drew, and this going public thing with Dr. Z? He'd warned her there would probably be consequences, and he couldn't guarantee her abductors would leave her alone. It was his theory, and he believed that was going to be the outcome, but he could be wrong.

After her last phone call, Phoebe became bored and asked Val where she was from. She asked if she had another job or if she was a full-time Lyft driver. It didn't seem a good idea to explain she was far from home, so she began a chain of lies. She put together a life she'd wished she'd lived, where she was a graduate of St. Mary's, and she taught chemistry to underprivileged youth so they could get into college and have careers. She didn't know what else to say so she said she was also a YouTuber who made DIY videos that helped people learn dance moves. She had to hum the songs herself to avoid copyright deactivation, but that was part of the charm of her videos. Before long, Phoebe was dropped off at a cafe, with Phoebe's life closer to the one Val had made up, and she was alone again, and driving to a UFO conference where Dr. Z would talk about her, and people would believe her and ask questions, and as anxious as she was about admitting the truth to the world, currently she was terrified the Grays would come for her and she'd miss everything.

She picked up a guy named Zach, who didn't try to talk to her at all, but he texted on his phone the whole time, so she had no idea what he was like or who he hung out with, but she was sure his was a safer and better life than any she could have, because even after coming clean about her experiences, even if the E.T.s really did leave her alone, she'd know they were still out there and she'd know what they had done to her, and in an instant they could be back, so she was never going to feel safe, as Zach was, even if Zach knew he was going to die someday, because he sure didn't act like it.

Then there was Rosa, and Charlie, and Mabel, and Mark. Some of them travelled with companions, some were on the way to meet companions. Always, they moved easily across town in uncomplicated ways that seemed worry-free and Val envied them because they'd been spared the things she knew to be real. They could laugh it off if someone ever told them about such beings, because those kinds of people were crazy, and crazy couldn't wiggle its way into their brains, not Rosa, Charlie, Mabel, or Mark. And they had no idea that the one who was driving them was one of those people, except Val knew she wasn't crazy, despite having doubted herself many times before. She was just unlucky to be chosen for some reason she couldn't explain, and Rosa, Charlie, Mabel, and Mark were lucky to be ignorant of the watchers and the visitors and they slept soundly at night while their driver tossed all night, burdened by the weight of what had been done to her.

hristie Lewis's demonstration was the highlight of the conference for Amy and Cher, who sat next to each other and chatted about the possibilities of who she would debut. They'd seen enough while they'd been here to know there were alien species that Christie had yet to represent in her art. Amy wanted to see someone angelic, though she knew depicting a creature of light in clay would require an extreme talent, so it might be too much to hope for. Cher imagined Christie molding one of the many species of reptilians, even with one of the shape-shifters in the audience, who would be called out by what Zeta showed Christie, and this imposter would get up to leave under some pretense, but Cher would know. Cher understood there were aliens among us. Whatever Jim had gone through, it was an effort to keep that reality suppressed.

Christie leaned forward on a stool with a lump of bright lemon clay on a throwing wheel in front of her. With her eyes closed, she held her hands up to indicate that she needed silence, and she straightened her back as she meditated and listened to a far-off voice. She smiled and seemed to understand something she hadn't ever considered. She opened her eyes suddenly, and she kneaded the lump of clay to soften it

"You know you're communicating with a Zeta because of the certainty of what is shown," she said. "Other species may not want to talk. They may think of us as a waste of time, although they may have very different concepts of time. It's like this: if we value time, that's enough. They may not want to give us something we think of as valuable, even if they don't see it that way. But a Zeta will talk. Zeta is only interested in the truth. You ask for truth; you'll get some truth."

The lump had become an elongated head, so it seemed she might make a conehead as a joke, but she rolled out appendages to stick on the face and the crowd understood she had been shown something insectoid. She made a double mandible with four protruding hooks, and she rolled out segments for antennae, to be placed when the visage was more complete.

"The Mantids are a very old and wise species," she said.

"I *knew* it!" someone shouted from the back.

Amy was disappointed but intrigued. Here was a creature she should probably know more about. Maybe she'd have the chance to ask Christie about Angels later, in The Interstellar Lounge.

When Jim saw that Dr. Z was on the schedule, he knew he had to go. This was his doctor, who would talk about Val's experiences, and Jim wanted to be there. He wanted the validation of an audience reacting to abductees. Luckily, Dr. Z's presentation followed the sculpture woman, and in a different room, so he snuck out and he knew the girls would stick around to chat Christie up over Vulcan mind melds. Cher had never heard of such beings and she sat ready, open to anything and eager to learn.

"Mantids are strong telepaths with the ability to manipulate others. They often control the Grays behind the scenes. They don't want to harm us but will abduct as part of a larger mission. They can see cosmic consequences we could only guess at. They can justify any perceived malevolence, and they act with impunity."

She took a sharp tool and dug lines to indicate large eyes and she made criss-cross lines over the surface of the eyes to make them look compound.

"You can talk to a Mantid. One may even take an interest in you over several years. But they may also keep information from you or they may choose not to respond to your questions."

A hand shot up.

"Yes?"

"Does he have a name?"

"Neither he nor she, this one goes by Gull, though it has used other names in other circumstances."

"Are you saying we shouldn't trust them?"

"If you find yourself in the presence of a Mantid, you are part of something you are helpless to change. They may use their power to alleviate your fear, or they may wipe clean any memory of the encounter. They are somewhat like royalty and require the same kind of caution and respect. You will know this intuitively, and whatever your mind has the urge to do, you'll be unable to run."

"I didn't think they actually looked like insects. I thought Insectoids were in a different class as Mantids altogether."

"They may or may not reveal their true form. Gull has shown Zeta his insect-like appearance, though you are quite right, the ones we think of as Insectoids think and behave in a more lowly way. An Insectoid can't hold you with its mind and it can't see intersecting fates. It might be intelligent and either apathetic toward you, or kind, but it has none of the majesty of the Mantid, and none of the charm."

"I want one!" Cher said.

"This Gull sculpture will be for sale on my website. It'll need to be fired and glazed, of course, so please allow two to three weeks before it ships."

Amy wanted one too, though she was afraid of it, and she was sure Jim wouldn't like it in their house. But she thought maybe it could protect him, and succumbing to its absolute authority was better than whatever the government was doing to him. He sat next to her and flipped through news headlines on his phone, disinterested. She wanted to shake him. She wanted him to see how there were extra-terrestrials powerful enough to help him, like the Zetas, and maybe this Mantid, Gull.

"Can you channel Gull?"

"Only if it wants to be channeled. Its mind is so powerful that I personally don't want to. Zeta will intervene on my behalf."

"Can we ask it something?"

"Go ahead."

"Were the Mayans right, but we're reading the calendar wrong?"

"There is always a catastrophic event on the horizon, one that can be pushed back with collective goodwill."

"Is that what happened in 2012?"

"More happened in 2012 than we can ever know."

"Like what?"

"..."

"Tell us."

"I'm sorry," Christie said. "I told you they can ignore you if they want. Is there another question?"

"Did we really go to the moon?"

"It depends on who you mean by 'we,' on what timeline, and whether you mean in a human-built rocket or something else."

"Sounds like a 'no'."

"It's never all-the-way 'no' with a Mantid," Christie said.

"Is God a woman?"

And while she continued to etch details into the clay face with giant eyes, Christie casually said, "Yes." And then she followed up with "Oh, wow. I wasn't expecting that."

r. Z was at the podium. Valery and one other abductee sat to his left, facing an audience that included Jim Clinton. As Dr. Z talked about her experiences, Val blushed. She was aware of all they'd done to her, but hearing it recounted in front of strangers was overwhelming. She was glad they'd given her a water bottle. She drank it before Dr. Z was done. He talked about the woman seated next to her, someone named Molly. Val suspected it wasn't her real name, though probably some of them thought the same about her. She wondered what name she might have chosen for herself. Dr. Z had introduced her to Molly before the talk, and while they shared abductee status, Val tried not to look at Molly while she was being talked about, but she stole glances as her experiences went into territory Val couldn't imagine. She couldn't help but pity Molly and to stare at her as she squirmed in her chair.

Dr. Z told everyone that Molly had been shown a hybrid baby and they told her it was hers. They had impregnated her and taken it from her before she began to show. When they returned with it, they wanted her to hold it and to breastfeed it, which was a barrage of conflicted emotions for her. She was repulsed by, but also loved the creature. She held the alien that was also her, and it was vulnerable and it needed her. The baby was a boy and it knew how to suckle. She remembered having dreams of being pregnant and suddenly she had been given a baby and she was breastfeeding. Hearing this was too much for Val and she wished Dr. Z had given her a Valium.

As the years went by, these kinds of experiences repeated for Molly. She'd spawned other hybrids and she'd had contact with her children as they grew up. There'd be a gangly preteen in a silver spacesuit with her thin blonde hair. They never smiled and they talked telepathically, so that she never heard her children's voices, even the babies cried telepathically when they cried at all.

All the while Molly had trouble keeping a job. She'd had sleepless nights and would go missing for long stretches, sometimes for more than a day. Everyone assumed she was on drugs so she didn't dare talk about what she suspected, and when she finally found Dr. Z she was relieved to know she wasn't crazy. Soon, she was terrified by what she was sure was real.

Today, her hybrid children were adults and they lived in an apartment in a nearby city. She often had to spend time with them to help them adapt. Although they'd lived on Earth, there was so much they didn't understand. They stood out as foreigners. They didn't know how to eat a sandwich. They couldn't see that it might be wrong to control someone's mind for fun or for gain. When the power or the cable went out she would be taken to them in a spaceship in the dark of night. Her children would hand her wads of cash and tell her to fix the problem. They were apathetic about most things human. They only became excited about some vague point in the future when a change would come and all would be revealed. Molly listened with trepidation because she hated being used and she imagined being used to exhaustion with nowhere to go.

"We'll all be together soon," they said, and this terrified her.

According to Dr. Z, what Molly had gone through was a pattern that he was starting to see, and more than anything Val didn't want this to happen to her. She already had a kid and that was hard enough. She couldn't imagine having a brood of them, as needy as that, and also able to control her with their minds.

Dr. Z introduced Val and told stories of her missing time. How she disappeared and turned up later, disoriented and afraid. Val understood the similarities between her story and where Molly's began. If this was allowed to progress on its own, she was surely headed there.

Dr. Z turned to Molly and Val and he told the audience they'd be happy to take questions. She knew it was just a phrase, but Val and Molly looked at each other and neither was happy. In front of any other audience, Val supposed they would try to trip her up, to discount her experiences, to make everyone think she was crazy, or lying, but these were believers who were more than certain that everything they'd been told had really happened.

Val opened a second water bottle and drank from it. She sat back and waited, because Molly had the more sensational story, so most of the questions would be for her. But a man with a gray beard and a kind of fisherman's vest with UFO insignia patches looked right at Val and said, "Have you considered getting a dog?"

"I've heard that might help," Val said, "but I don't know what kind."

"A big one," the man said. "Will cost more to feed, but worth it in terms of protection: German Shepherd, Akita, Rottweiler, Giant Schnauzer."

Another question came to her from a woman under an Arizona Diamondbacks baseball cap, "Have you gotten a DNA test for your son?"

"He's mine," Val said. "I'm sure."

"But I've heard there are genetic markers common to experiencers. It may provide some sense of relief, to know one way or another."

"Whether or not they're coming for him?" Val said. "I doubt there's a test for that."

"It's a theory," Dr. Z intervened, "in the community, that experiencers could be identified from genetic markers, and also that alien DNA could be found."

The woman in the baseball cap nodded in agreement. She knew Dr. Z from previous talks. They'd been coming here for years and had seen the same speakers.

"The fear," Dr. Z explained to the audience, "is that the government will use this information to identify experiencers, which might come with some form of discrimination, or they could all be detained."

"And do we want Google to have a database of alien DNA?" the woman added.

Val realized that the questions weren't so much for her as they were for the audience members to participate in the larger discussion, to proclaim their beliefs and to show off what they knew.

"I had no idea," Val said. "I don't plan to get one."

What she didn't say, and what she was thinking, was that all of this sounded very expensive, getting some kind of police dog and paying for DNA tests. She was barely getting by driving for Lyft as it was. She knew that even if she got a better job, she wouldn't be able to keep it.

"My boys wouldn't let anyone near them to take a sample," Molly said.

"Are they all boys?"

"There was a girl but she refuses to live with them. We don't see her. I assume she's up there somewhere."

"Do you miss her?"

"I've never gotten to know her, but in a weird way I miss her. Yes, I do."

Val saw that Molly was better at performing for them, that she sort of enjoyed the attention and the validation. The whole reason Val agreed to come was that she wanted something helpful to come from this, while Molly seemed at peace with what was a terrible situation.

"How many fingers do they have?"

"Did they let you fly the ship?"

"Did they show you a star chart?"

"Did they show you a vision of the future?"

"What kind of suits did they wear?"

"Did you see any technology that, if used for good, could save humanity?"

"Did they talk about God?"

"Do they come from other dimensions?"

"Do they work in sterile environments? Are they afraid of disease?"

"Have you ever seen them eat? Do they like our food?"

"Do they come to you in dreams?"

"Do you sometimes know things you shouldn't know?"

"Are you a musician? Have they inspired your songs?"

"Are there colors we can't see?"

Molly and Val fielded questions as best they could, but most of what the audience wanted to know was beyond the scope of their experiences.

Jim Clinton stood in the audience. He had been standing for some time when Dr. Z finally called on him.

"Do you ever feel like, no matter what you do, you can't make them go away?"

"Yes."

"That they've shown up to punish you for something you did that no one knows about, not even yourself."

"Yes, that's it."

"And they don't even look like aliens, they look like short people in masks."

"No, they look like aliens."

"And they've got you drugged up on something and they're telling you they'll kill you if you talk."

"That hasn't been my experience," Molly said.

"They don't tell you not to remember," Val said, "you just wake up somewhere with your clothes on inside out and no memory of where you'd been."

"But I remember," Jim said, "I feel like they want me to remember."

"We should chat afterwards," Dr. Z said, as a way of wrapping up, because there were other speakers waiting to use the room. "We'll be out in the hall if anyone else wants to talk."

A third of the room cleared out as the rest stayed for the next presentation, an Air Force Airman who claimed to be actively enrolled in their remote viewing program.

As the girls went for drinks with Christie Lewis and Jim Clinton went to listen to some experiencers, Tommy found himself drawn to a presentation about cattle mutilations. All this time, he'd imagined the ones up there would judge him for eating meat. Yet, as he sat listening to the details of what could only be described as the bizarre and ritual slaughter of cattle in the middle of the night, with lasers from UFOs, he felt a sickness in the pit of his stomach. Because here were aliens who left the meat to rot in fields but they took the blood, the tongues and lips, the genitals. He couldn't imagine what they might want, but he listened in horror as the small man at the podium described a species of aliens who fed by soaking in vats of a serum made from cow's blood.

In his short time as a vegetarian, he had developed a distaste for blood. He didn't like walking past the packaged meats in the grocery store, and he couldn't imagine how many cows it took to keep all the fast-food joints open on so many corners in even the smallest of cities. While the black-and-white photos of the cattle lying in fields with the bones of their teeth and jaws exposed was terrifying and inexplicable, so was the nearly incomprehensible numbers of cattle consumed on sesame seed buns each day. Seeing the shocking images of the mutilated cattle and hearing the theories of what the E.T.s wanted with the blood and parts was disturbing even for those who had seen the pictures before. But we also killed and consumed them, so were we any better? And this awareness, from Tommy Trump, who'd had a lifetime of gleefully grilling meats, had suddenly upended his sense of stability and his acceptance of the existence of the UFO pilots. Because maybe they weren't so enlightened and "good." Maybe they had bloodlust, and if so, maybe they could egg us on toward war. And who was to say that there weren't vats of blood-serum drained from humans, because there were a lot of missing children. All the shocking unexplained events met in a kind of simple brutal logic that Tommy didn't want to think about. He much preferred the higher vibration of vegetarianism and the ethical awareness of shining with goodness in our time together.

But the images kept coming. Here were twenty dead cattle with their faces, eyes, and tails removed. Here was a cow with an empty middle where there was nothing left but a ribcage. What earthly animal might do this? What mythical animal? What alien or secret government agenda might justify it?

There was an artist's rendering of a formation of saucers zapping unsuspecting cows with lasers. And there was an artist's rendering of a Gray alien soaking in a clear tube of translucent pink liquid. And while the uptick was slight, the small slit of a mouth appeared to be smiling. Tommy couldn't fathom any intelligent creature being happy to be doing these things, until he remembered his own cookouts not too many months ago, and he nearly wept with remorse. He held his head in his hands so that he'd gotten the attention of the presenter.

"These are graphic images," the man at the podium said, "but it's important that we understand what has been happening. Because without the photos, no one would believe it, and they'd ridicule us when we told the truth."

Next was an aerial view of a crop circle that appeared within a mile of a cattle mutilation event, and while many interpreted the symbols as having occult significance, the speaker pointed out a way of seeing the crop circle that tabulated two dates, the night the mutilation occurred, and a future date coupled with a crowd of Grays, as if to foretell the time of their mass arrival.

"We need to be prepared for, and to prevent the risk of starvation that would occur if all of our cattle suddenly vanished," the man said.

Tommy understood the rightness of his own vegetarianism. And he believed it was something the space visitors had encouraged him to do. Because if they wanted all the cow's lips, and the cow's blood, then his vegetarian diet was preparing him for their arrival. If he and people like the man at the podium could somehow convince everyone of the rightness of this lifestyle, then the supply chain of beef would have been replaced with veggie burgers on a grand scale, and they could live together in harmony with these alien visitors, who were coming whether we were ready or not.

With that, Tommy shuffled out to join Cher and Amy at The Interstellar Lounge. They shared a booth where Christie Lewis had had a drink with them, but she'd already left. "Werewolves of London" played on the jukebox and it was enough to lift Tommy's spirits. The girls were giddy because of their new friendship with a star on the UFO circuit, and because Cher had ordered no fewer than seven alien heads from her. She knew Tommy would let out an exasperated gasp when she told him. She had tried to whittle it down but couldn't. In order to truly represent the intelligentsia of the near cosmos, Cher would need all seven.

Tommy looked over the menu, which was printed on un-laminated orange card stock, with burgers and chicken fingers given UFO names for the conference, so that when it was over these temporary menus would be tossed out and The Broken Spoke would return to its regular state of operation. They did serve a veggie burger but Tommy wanted meat. He knew now that the UFO pilots not only wouldn't judge him for eating beef, but they did so themselves.

"I'll have the Area 51 with cheese," he told the waitress, and Cher cocked her head and stared at him. She'd eaten one, but she'd gotten used to Tommy, the picky eater. They'd started driving to the Thai place in South Bend where he could get any of the dishes with tofu. He was tired of explaining everything to all the wait staff at the restaurants in Nappanee.

"They eat meat," Tommy told Cher, "at least some of them."

"No?"

"With their small mouths?" Amy said. "Do they even have teeth?"

"They absorb it," Tommy said.

"We all like to imagine they're better," Amy said, "because of their technology."

"Absorb it how?" Cher wanted to know.

"They bathe in beef blood."

"That is disgusting," Cher said. "Why is everyone here so happy about them?"

A man in a brown leather jacket like Indiana Jones who had been eavesdropping in the next booth turned around and said, "Because they made us. They are our gods."

"Like Greek gods?" Cher said.

"Earlier," he said, "but yes."

"Prove it," Cher added.

"It's all on the Sumerian clay tablets. The Annunaki made us in a lab with the DNA from apes and they gave us math, language, and agriculture."

"What are you talking about?"

"The fertile crescent. Agriculture appeared entire, from nowhere, and on the tablets they explain it was from the gods, the ones from the sky, the Annunaki."

"Christie Lewis makes one of them," Amy said.

"I know," Cher said. "I didn't get one. Do you think I should?"

"That stuff in the Bible about making use of the animals?" the man said. "It comes from them. They gave us the seed and the plow. They gave us husbandry."

"Then they left?"

"But they're coming back," he said. "I have a theory about when they're coming back."

Tommy's burger was set in front of him with a heap of fries and he poured out ketchup and stared at the plate unsure of what to do. The fries were still too hot and the burger glistened with grease. Here, before him, was the product of a gift from the gods, across the millennia.

"All the old religions," the man said. "They came from there."

"And when are they returning?" Tommy said. He finally lifted his burger and took a bite, which tasted good, but not as good as he remembered.

"We can posit that each transit occurred simultaneously with a historic catastrophic event, say: Noah's Flood."

"I though that was just a story," Cher said.

"No," Amy said. "There's a podcast about it."

"Just tell us when," Tommy said.

"Possibly in the next fifty years," he said, "but probably some time in the next four hundred."

"In the next four hundred years?" Tommy said, and he took another bite. He wished he'd gone ahead and gotten the veggie burger, what had they called it? The Majestic 12-*something*? 12 ounce?

"In the grand scheme of things," he said, "that's pretty soon."

"I suppose I can wait on getting an Annunaki," Cher said.

"Where's Jim?" Tommy said.

"He went to some talk," Amy said. "We're meeting up later."

In the hall, Dr. Z was with Val and Molly when Jim came up to them. Dr. Z nodded in recognition of one of his patients, but he also didn't want to give Jim away. The idea that our government was trying to confuse the whole abduction phenomenon by planting false memories was too complicated to bring up at a talk like this, and he was glad Jim kept quiet about it. He handed Jim his card, to pretend he didn't know him, and he explained how regression worked.

Jim stepped close to Val, so that he was in her space and he stared down at her cleavage. Amy hadn't given Jim any hotel sex, though she kept hinting at it. Seeing Val onstage and listening to Dr. Z talk about her paralyzed and naked on an examination table in a spaceship gave him a hard-on that he pointed at her and she didn't back away. Val believed in fate and maybe this man had been brought to her.

"We can catch up later," she said to Molly.

To Dr. Z she said, "I feel dirty after all that. I need a shower."

To Jim she said, "Come with me. We should talk."

Jim walked closely behind her like he had no say in the matter. Except he did. He knew he was married. He knew he could bump into Amy on his way up to this stranger's room. Or his neighbors, Tommy and

Cherise. But he followed anyway. He was aroused and it made him aggressive and stupid.

Once they were alone in her room, Val took off her clothes and she went into the bathroom to shower. Jim wanted to follow her but he waited. He paced in the dim room as the air conditioner unit below the heavy orange curtain buzzed and he got the notion to leave without saying anything. To pretend nothing had happened. Then he heard her crying over the sound of the shower and he knocked twice before going in.

She sat on the bottom of the bathtub with hot water cascading down on her and she sobbed. The room was filled with steam and Jim was annoyed by it, and annoyed by this woman who needed to pull herself together. If the UFOs had a plan that included bringing Jim and Val together, here they were, and they needed to go ahead and get on with it.

He took a terry cloth robe from the hook on the door, leaned into the bathtub, turned off the shower, and tossed the robe at her in a way he realized may have seemed cold. He reached down to help her up and once she was situated, with the robe on, and she wiped her face with the sleeve, he led her back out to the bed.

They had both been unsettled by the story of Molly, who had been used as a breeder, and Jim knew the kindest thing he could do for Val, who had been suffering because of her abductions, just as he had, only worse—he knew that what she needed was a baby, a human baby, and here he was to give one to her.

So that once the covers were pulled back, and Val's robe was opened, Jim pulled his pants down and he moved quickly. He didn't pull out, which he always did with Amy, though he wasn't thinking about her. He imagined a star child, his own human astronaut baby, who the UFO pilots would surely take up and examine, but it was better than letting Val be the victim of some kind of hybrid breeding program where she'd be made to raise freaks who would control her and use her up. Jim saved her from that. At least this was what he chose to believe as he came inside her.

When he got up, she reached for him as if she wanted him to stay, but he shook his head, he put his pants back on, and he left her alone in her room.

There would be consequences for this encounter, but he assumed they would all be good, and he would keep the memory tucked away, just as he had with his abductions, which he couldn't admit were real, not even fake-real.

Feeling manly, Jim wanted a smoke, an urge he never succumbed to, except he may as well now, and he went to The Interstellar Lounge to bum one.

Amy and Cher sat with Christie Lewis and before his wife saw him, Christie Lewis got up and she came over to Jim on the other side of the bar.

"Come with me," she said, "we need to talk."

Jim had paid too much for her art and there were alien heads in his living room that he resented. He wouldn't walk through that part of the house at night if he could avoid it, because he didn't want them staring back at him.

Christie pulled him to an empty stairwell where they were alone and she said, "I know what they've been doing to you, and you have to believe me that they're not who they seem to be."

Jim searched his mind for what she might be talking about. He thought maybe she meant Cher and Tommy, but that couldn't be it.

Christie recognized the look of confusion on his face and she said, "Your abductions. The Zetas have told me about them."

Jim felt a sinking in his gut because here was proof that they were real.

"They're not real," Christie Lewis said. "They're human agents, and they're messing with you to scare you."

Jim remembered flashes of those nightmarish experiences and he remembered humans in uniforms with guns being present. He remembered never taking off in a ship or seeing the outside of a ship. He remembered wandering past curtains into fog and into the woods, and he knew what Christie had told him was true. They wore masks and they drugged him with something to make him believe he was abducted. This was a relief and a new terror all at once. Because it confirmed his certainty that UFOs didn't exist, but it meant he was the target of something more sinister and more dangerous. And it meant that if he had been pushed toward the woman he'd impregnated, then it may have been the U.S. government who wanted him to do so, to prevent the aliens he didn't believe in from doing what they'd done to that other woman. So that maybe his government, even if they were working in the shadows, might be working for the greater good. And he couldn't even remember that woman's name. He was as confused and mixed up as if he had been given whatever drug they'd used. He sat on the stairs and looked up at Christie who held his hands to reassure him.

"What else did they say?" he said.

"That's all I know."

Jim was relieved she didn't seem to know about who he'd been with, and he asked, "What do I do?"

"I don't know," Christie said. "You can try meditating to open a channel, and if they come for you again, call out to the Zetas for help."

"Will they help me?"

"If it's the right thing to do, and if they're able to, they will."

"That's a lot of 'ifs'."

"There's always a lot of 'ifs'."

Jim got up and he went back to the bar. He could hear the crowd noise and he recognized the piano riff of "Werewolves of London" as Christie gave Jim a cigarette and a book of matches with her website address on it before she went off on her own. Jim walked past the bar to go outside with his cigarette, and when Jim came back into the bar he acted like he'd only just arrived. He needed a drink and who better to enjoy a Vulcan mind meld with than his wife and his neighbors? Tommy was with the girls and he was eating a real hamburger.

In the back of Arnie's prop, Amy wore aviator goggles and a headset with a mic. Arnie had strapped her in, and they rolled to the end of the runway where he throttled up. As they took to the sky she was in awe of the Ozark Mountains and the bright noonday sun.

Arnie had a diagram of his maneuvers and he warned Amy that there would be a lot of diving and climbing, and some rolls, but he was trying to reproduce the symbols from the photos she'd given him, and that's what was required. They'd talked on the phone after his Fourth of July stunt and Amy offered constructive criticism. Here the loop should be tighter. Here the line should arc more. Arnie had said then that a lot depended on her vantage point. These were three-dimensional scribbles and their appearance would change with the point of observation.

Arnie gestured at the conference hotel where there was a small crowd outside.

"Enjoying the weather?" he said.

"They're playing Pokemon Go," Amy explained. "There are new monsters for the conference."

"Let's give them something to look at," Arnie said, and he dipped down to within a few hundred feet of the ground where he activated the smoke to draw his first line.

Amy watched as the crowd looked up and a few were pointing. She supposed they expected an advertisement, or a marriage proposal, and she felt glad inside. This crowd would soon witness the facsimile of an actual UFO message. They were slated to talk tomorrow, and Amy had flyers she would put up around the hotel with the tantalizing remark, "Seen this?" along with Cher's best zoomed-in photo of the message in the sky. Amy, Tommy, Arnie, Jim, and Cher would all talk about their experiences, there would be a crowd who had come to see them, and lines of communication would be opened that very well might lead to answers.

Arnie said, "This next one is steep," and Amy's stomach dropped as they took a sharp dive. She was laughing as they leveled off.

"This is better than a roller coaster!"

"And slightly more death-defying."

A new crowd filtered out of The Interstellar Lounge, everyone was watching, with several of them pointing.

This was a really good idea Arnie had and Amy was glad she'd talked him into doing it on the Fourth of July, because this was better than his first draft of alien letters, and among all the life-long believers down on the ground, there had to be someone who had a best-guess at what it said.

After Airman Riley's presentation he opened the floor for questions and a hand shot up. A man in an aluminum foil hat, as a joke, stood up, though they reconsidered if it was a joke when he said, "I thought you were going to talk about chemtrails. I came here to learn about chemtrails."

Airman Riley didn't know how to respond. He had been vague with his conference submission because that was his agreement with the Major. They would let him talk as long as his audience was small. If Riley wanted to be insistent about going, they'd let him see how the truth died with a whimper.

But someone else in the audience said, "You should have been here four years ago when chemtrails were all the rage. Talk to me later. I can fill you in."

Airman Riley supposed, with his special abilities, that it would be easy for him to find out about chemtrails. He could simply spirit walk from hangar to hangar and look around to find out what was going on. But here was someone in the audience who claimed to know, and Airman Riley was curious. So he said, "Come on up here. You tell us what's going on."

"I'm not really much of a speaker," he said. "I don't have any slides."

"No really," Riley said. "Come up here and tell us."

So the man walked up to the podium. He wore a blue blazer with a skinny red DEVO tie, his lapels covered with buttons and pins, a few of them Riley recognized: Rush, Dead Kennedys, Dennis Kucinich for President, a crossed-out NAFTA, and a hand-drawn Devil's Tower with the inscription, "We are not alone."

He cleared his throat, lowered the mic, and said, "Chemtrails are real. There's an Air Force training manual, an Air Force insignia, inflated pilot salaries for regular and repetitive flight missions, and high concentrations of crystalized aluminum and barium from ground and water samples taken all over. It's in the soil, in the lakes and rivers, in the air we breathe. And there are three likely theories regarding the purpose of all that artificial cloud cover: a reflective layer to slow global warming; a matrix for a three-dimensional NORAD radar defense system; and a third, more sinister theory that involves trans-humanistic mapping and a behavior control mechanism linked to 5G radio towers, at the behest of fourth-dimension demonic entities, which even I don't buy, though there's more evidence for that theory than the others, if you want to believe it."

The man started out with a sure sense of what was being hidden, and he'd won over the audience until he'd talked himself into a corner. It was hard not to go for the sensational once he'd started, and it was hard to know what was disinformation. Was the global warming story a cover-up for a mind-control program begun by demonic entities, or was the demonic entities story a cover-up for the enhanced NORAD radar? He had no way of knowing, and Riley wanted to take the aluminum foil hat from the first man's head and ball it up, because he knew that as crazy as it sounded, none of it was really that crazy. Airman Riley had just spoken with absolute authority about an out-of-body spy program that he had first-hand personal experience with, one that most scientific-minded Americans would immediately dismiss as made-up. Maybe the Major planted the idea of coming here, and this outcome—that Riley wasn't as believable as a guy in an actual aluminum foil hat—was what he'd wanted him to learn. Though the manipulation of Riley's story probably went higher than the Major who might be a pawn of disinformation, telling his wife everything he knew when they were in bed at night, so she'd tell her sister, who would spill it to their second cousin, who even the Major knew had a habit of spending way too much time posting to online message boards.

As the talk got away from him, Airman Riley went to the back of the room and slipped out into the hall. He had said what he had come here to say and taking questions may have opened him up to giving away too much. He was disinclined to lie and he didn't want to dance around the topic. He had stood in front of a room of believers and he'd given them the truth of the past three years. So that despite what he knew, he also understood that there must be more that our government was involved with. Most only had access to specific compartmentalized knowledge with no idea what anyone else might be doing. What Riley knew was harder to control, because he had the habit of walking about.

Riley didn't want a drink and he didn't want to go back to his room, so he went to another room in this same hotel, where he'd seen a Nubian Alien with a tall afro who wore a medallion on a gold chain and funky moon boots. Riley had said what he wanted to say, and now he was ready to listen.

Jim Clinton sat at the end of a long table next to Cherise Trump, who was next to Tommy, who was next to the pilot, with Amy at the podium with a projector screen behind her that showed Cher's famous shot of the message in the sky and the title of the talk in a royal blue cursive font across the top of the photo, "They're Trying to Tell Us Something." Jim scanned the audience that was larger than he could have imagined, for familiar faces. Were there army grunts among them who had kidnapped and drugged him? Were there Zetas disguised as humans? He didn't know yet what he was going to say, but he brought a legal pad and a pen to jot some things down. So far all he'd written was, "Are they real?" with extra question marks down the page. He'd left more room to write if he thought of something while listening to Amy, but he couldn't get past that initial question. Because he still didn't know.

Amy was the one who'd organized all this and she'd wanted to speak out about what they'd seen for a long time. She'd had the idea for the website. She'd contacted Christie Lewis and bought alien busts from her. She got Arnie to sky-write the message. And she'd sent in the conference proposal. As much as this whole thing was anyone's, it was Amy's. And though it was her photo up there on the screen, Cher was keenly aware of how much of their mutual experience was thanks to Amy. Cher crossed and uncrossed her legs. She folded her arms. She even gave a long exhale as Amy recounted what it was like to be in the middle of Nowheresville Indiana and look up to see a message from an alien civilization.

Jim was distracted by Cher's fidgeting and they were seated so close together that he became aroused by her. He'd had sex with someone he wasn't married to recently, and it was easy. He opened the woman's bathrobe and that was it. He was awash in Cher's perfume and he drew doodles of UFOs on his notepad to try to refocus. He remembered that Cher would have let him have her just to spite Amy, and if they were alone again, he wouldn't be able to trust himself. Especially since he didn't like this version of Amy who was eating up the attention with dramatic sweeps of her arms and pregnant pauses in her story. She was taking too long, Cher was miserable inside, and Jim wanted to put a baby in her to keep her ineligible for the covert alien-hybrid breeding program. Jim leaned back in his chair to get a better look at Cher's body, and he ogled her in her magenta yoga pants and oversized pale blue Oxford shirt, which Amy didn't notice because she was in the middle of performing her story, and the pilot didn't notice because he was next and he was getting nervous, but Tommy did notice and he shot Jim a questioning glare. So Jim sat back up in his chair and went back to doodling, like he'd been caught at nothing, because he doubted Tommy would actually say anything.

And when Amy sat back down to a smattering of applause, the pilot stood at the podium to repeat a shorter version of the solo talk he'd already given: "In all my years of flying I never saw anything weird until after I was hired to reproduce these symbols in the sky. And then like we'd called out to them, I saw a small red UFO, followed by F-16s, so I knew it was real.

"It had mass. It was reflective. And there was no exhaust. No visible engine or cockpit. But man, that thing could move."

Amy forwarded the slide to Arnie's drawing of the small red craft, and as crude as it was, this audience was familiar with the amateur artistic abilities of experiencers. His story elicited as much excitement as Amy's, if not more, because a pilot lent a certain amount of authority to a UFO sighting. Pilots knew about flight, they had a scientific view of things, and they risked their careers if they came out to talk like this. There was more of Cher's photography, taken on the ground as Amy and Arnie were skywriting above the conference hotel, and Jim gave Cher a thumbs-up to acknowledge her steady hand and ability to get the hotel in the frame, to give a scale reference for the symbols, which then helped to indicate the size of the original craft, which was probably at least as big as the hotel. It made Tommy feel like a mouse looking at a picture of a cat on the projector screen, so he didn't notice when Cher smiled back at Jim, and Jim rested his hand on her shoulder, which was soft and feminine and the touch didn't last long, though he wanted it to.

Meanwhile, Arnie dissected his maneuvers as a way of illustrating the three-dimensional quality of the symbols, and he stepped away from the podium occasionally to make dry-erase ink drawings on a white board that showed each symbol from various points of view.

"It looks different on the ground than to someone in the sky. So maybe it says one thing to us, another thing to another UFO, and something else to someone farther away."

"Assuming it says anything at all," Jim mumbled and Cher laughed, and she sidled her pink Adidas up next to his Florsheim, so their feet were touching. Here they were playing footsie, with Tommy there, and Amy there. And with this slight gesture Jim was glad with uncontrollable desire, because he was pretty sure now that all he had to do was get Cher alone.

Apparently, everyone had a question for the pilot. There were questions about making the symbols, questions about his later encounter, about the F-16s, about Round-Up, and about chemtrails. Arnie could have stood at the podium all day, except Amy was losing her patience and she cut him off to give the floor to Tommy, who was a salesman, though it wasn't at all clear what he was selling.

"What do they eat?" Tommy said, and no one was sure if this was a rhetorical question or if he really wanted to know.

If he'd done his research he'd have uncovered stories of Grays soaking up nutrients through their thin skins while taking baths, or of them drinking blood like vampires. There were reptilians who ate children, or molested children, the stories got confused, but the consumption of human flesh, and/ or the spiritual consumption of human fear and misery was something the reptilians were somehow mixed up in. The Annunaki drank beer out of clay vessels with straws, but beyond that there was confusion about what they liked to eat. Lambs and goats were roasted for them, or offered to them. So maybe if Tommy had done his research, he still would have had questions.

"Unless they're made of light, which they aren't, they have to eat. So what do they eat?"

There was silence, then a commotion as people stirred in their seats. They had expected some kind of presentation. They had thought he would provide his own answers, but he kept on.

"The spacesuits we hear about are always skin-tight, and thin. No one talks about toilets or refrigerators on their craft. So what do they eat?"

And finally, someone spoke up. Like many of the men in the audience he was overweight and wore a baseball cap too low on the brow. He said, "The Grays are actually biological robots—Ebens, or biological entities. We know this now. It's been reported many times from various sources working in underground facilities."

Once they understood they'd been given permission to reply, several others spoke up.

"I've heard they like cotton candy."

"Anything sweet really. Sugar is hard to come by in space."

"It has to be a liquid. They don't have teeth and their mouths are very small."

"Actually, their mouths are vestigial. Same as their genitals, or lack thereof. They can't speak or eat or shit as far as we know. Their bodies have adapted to, or been engineered to simply fly around in saucers from place to place."

"Would they judge us," Tommy asked, "for being eaters? For eating burgers with cheese?"

"They already think we're primitive. They communicate at such a rapid speed that talking to us is like explaining a computer program to a toddler. We aren't built to really get it."

"But do they judge us? Do they want us to change? Do they want us to be more like them?"

"These are good questions," Amy said, and she scooted him away from the podium and back to his seat because she saw his presentation was no presentation at all and was going nowhere.

Cher was up next and she was ready to talk about the rewards of meditation when she recognized Airman Riley in the audience. He'd shown up during her meditations, though she'd never met him in the flesh and here he was. He'd come to her talk.

As remarkable as this was, what was even more incredible was that seated next to Riley was a black alien, an African from outer space, a hip funky disco extra-terrestrial with a message of peace and love, a Soul Train UFO pilot and party galaxy ambassador from Venus. He was exactly who she wanted depicted in clay to round out her collection of alien busts, and Christie Lewis sat in this audience too. If she could just get everyone together she'd pay as much as $2,500 for a decent-sized sculpture. She was so enthralled with this idea that she forgot all about her talk.

Amy prompted her, "Ahem."

"I've seen you before," Cher said to no one in particular. "And I'm happy to see you here as well."

"Talk about the pictures," Amy said. "Do you have any advice about photographing UFOs with phone cameras?"

Cher took her phone out of her pocket. "It's an iPhone 7 but honestly the Samsung Galaxy is probably better."

"Do you want to say anything about the experience?"

"Please, no one leave afterwards. I need to talk to you."

"Is that it?"

"I think so."

And so it was Jim's turn and he still didn't know what he believed or what he wanted to say. Amy sensed this by his far-off look and if putting Cher in front of a microphone was a bad idea, Jim could certainly come off worse.

"I don't believe in UFOs," Jim said.

"But you *saw* one," Amy interrupted. There was an image of it projected on the screen behind him, taken with Cher's iPhone 7, though she thought a Samsung Galaxy might do better.

"There's a group of humans who want us to believe all this nonsense, and they're doing it so we'll have sex with each other."

Amy turned bright red. They'd been here three nights already and while she knew he expected sex, and that she'd promised him sex, she'd had a good excuse each night. Everything and everyone at the Ozarks Conference had been so invigorating that she was too tired, or too drunk, or too excited and she dozed off unintentionally each night as Jim waited up eager and expectant. Sleeping three nights with her in a hotel bed without sex had gone to his head. He'd gone insane with lust and had no idea what he was saying.

"They act out alien abductions on us and plant ideas in our heads. The government will deny it, because it's a secret program, but they're practicing mind control."

Airman Riley nodded as Jim spoke because he happened to know this was true, but he also knew that aliens existed, because he was seated next to one, and that was the true purpose of the covert fake-abduction program, to keep recognition of the real ones questionable. Riley knew that they did all they did to poor Jim Clinton just to keep everyone in doubt. And it worked, because here he was trying to impregnate Earth women and talking nonsense to a room of believers.

As Jim talked about his experiences, which were as real and as traumatic as a true alien abduction, someone in the back stood up and shouted, and it was the one word that could sink Amy's panel. As much as she loved being here among like-minded believers, this one divisive word put their entire discussion at risk of being dismissed and of her never being invited back, because what the man shouted was, "Disinformation!" Jim and Amy and Cher and Arnie and Tommy were suddenly suspected of being mouthpieces for the government, who didn't want us to know, or to believe, or to ask questions, and Amy slumped in her chair and nearly cried, because with that one word all her hard work may as well have been thrown in the trash. All she wanted was to get out the truth and her stupid husband ruined it. He'd been fighting her all along over this and she couldn't believe she'd ever loved him. It didn't matter what else he said now, and it didn't matter what she'd promised him to get him to come along, there wasn't going to be any hotel sex on their last night here and not any anywhere else or anytime in the near future. Jim had fucked it up big time and he'd better acknowledge that as soon as they were alone together, because she wanted to murder him, and she was pretty sure she'd be justified in doing so, so long as her jury was made up of a collection of her Ozark UFO Conference peers. All but the ones who saw her as a disinformation agent, which might all of a sudden be a lot, and she absolutely did not deserve it.

When Jim was done spewing nonsense, he sat next to Cher and tried to put his arm around her, but she got up quickly to go find Christie Lewis, just as Tommy had gotten up to go find someone who would sympathize with his eating dilemma. Amy and Jim and Arnie remained in their seats on the panel, without speaking to each other, and when Jim looked up at Amy she refused to return his gaze, so he knew he was in trouble, and he knew he deserved it, but what he thought he'd done wrong was not what Amy thought he'd done wrong, so when it came time to have that fight, he would be best to keep his mouth shut and to let her attack first. Meanwhile Cher was pulling Christie Lewis through the crowd to try to find the Nubian as everyone filed out. And someone came up to Arnie and said, loud enough for everyone else at the table to hear, "What if those symbols are a mind virus, a thought plague, a parasitic brain worm?"

Amy was furious with Jim and she told him so. In the hall after their talk, as conference attendees came and went she said he'd embarrassed her and she berated him.

"All you had to do," she said, "was talk about what we saw. You didn't have to say you believed in Martians. Just say you saw what you saw."

"I don't know what we saw."

"But you saw *something*."

Jim was distracted because of all of the people around them. More accurately, he was distracted by the women. He watched their butts sway as they passed in flowing Bohemian summer skirts. He remarked on all the colors and styles of hair, the tips often colored blue, pink, or purple. He felt a tug in his chest as he couldn't help himself but stare wherever there was cleavage. He was even drawn to where the hallway corners were rounded out into curves in this hotel, or where the light fixtures seemed to him to have overtly feminine shapes, and he needed to sit down. He'd been made to speak to an audience, which was well out of his comfort zone, and his nerves hadn't settled. He wanted to fuck everything around him as his wife became increasingly annoyed at the way he didn't seem to listen while she told him what he should have said.

He said, "I'm sorry." He said, "I'm not good at this." He said, "I told you I didn't want to do it."

And she said, "What the hell was that? You don't believe in UFOs but you *do* believe the U.S. Army has singled you out for harassment?"

"I didn't say it was the Army."

"Jim, what is going on?"

"Something has been happening to me," he said, "and I don't feel in control."

"Come on," she said, and she pulled him by the hand to the elevator, where miraculously, despite all the people in the halls on the last day of the conference, they were alone once the doors had shut.

"I know what you need," she said, and she embraced him.

In their room, she took off her clothes and told him to get in the bed. She gave off a whiff of nervous perspiration because of the presentation, but he was outright sweating. She went to the bathroom, brought back a towel, and she dabbed him off.

"It's lust," she said. "It's easy to fix. We can do this, shower, and go out to meet the Trumps for drinks."

"I don't want to see Cher," Jim said. "Can we stay in the room and keep going?"

"We should celebrate," Amy said. "We spoke to a room full of UFO experts and they believed us. We belong here. The Trumps did it too. We all did."

"Someone said it was disinformation," Jim said. "They could be right."

"They don't accuse you of that unless they really believe you." Amy was feeling better. "I was upset at first," she said, "but I think it's okay. I don't think he was in the majority opinion."

"What if they made me one? We don't know."

"You need to relax," she said. "You need sex."

Airman Riley stood at the podium with the projector off. He wanted to tell the audience all minds were connected, that the mind extended beyond the body. We're used to ourselves and we like staying in. We're not used to reaching out. Our hearts become overwhelmed if we feel everything, and our brains can't process it, but we're an expanse. We stretch out like nerve fibers, with tiny gaps between us where electricity flows.

He wanted to say that communicating with each other in this way was no different than communicating with far off aliens. At our core it's feelings and images that we express. The simplest emotions, when projected out, can heal. Anxiety, fear, anger, hate: we can help each other overcome negativity by projecting love, acceptance, respect. We are a young people recently welcomed to the galactic pantheon and we have so much to learn, so much to gain, so much to give. Every relationship is beneficial to both, and every conversation renews. We can go boldly without rocket fuel. And we can listen without a radio antenna array.

The Major was in the audience as Riley expected. What came out of Airman Riley's mouth at his talk, billed as "Remote Viewing Secrets of an Insider," sounded a lot like generalized hippy-dippy yoga enthusiasm.

He said, "The key to everything is meditation."

He said, "The deeper you go, the farther you go."

He said, "We can enter or exit through the chakras."

He said, "The planet has chakras too."

He said, "Buenos Aires is the throat. San Francisco is the root. So we've got it upside down. Because there is no up or down in space."

But UFOs fly upright wherever they are, instinctively knowing the ups and downs of wherever they are, the ships alive and with consciousness. They reach out to the stars, as our minds do, and they know the quickest path, free of gravity in those instances. He wanted to say more about UFOs but his mouth was dry. He paused to drink water from the bottle they'd provided him, and he was still thirsty. So he drank, and he forgot about UFOs. He forgot about the agents he saw when he went walking about where the Major had told him to go.

The Major was in the audience with his hand up, and he said, "I thought you were going to talk about Chemtrails."

Amy was right, and Jim felt calm again, post-coital. They joined the Trumps in The Interstellar Lounge and drank Vulcan mind melds, Tommy with a veggie burger and Cher with a juicy steak. The bar was less busy, with many of the conference attendees having checked out to go home already, though it was still loud, with enthusiasm everywhere as another year at Ozarks was in the books.

Tommy was glad to have his horizons widened, still unsure about the sustenance problem in deep space but glad for himself that he'd settled back into his own quirky brand of vegetarianism, where he might eat a sausage on any given day and he didn't really care that his veggie burger was cooked on the same griddle as the beef patties.

Cher was happy to see Amy and she thanked her for being the one to make it all happen: the website, the conference, and putting her in touch with Christie Lewis, who she'd commissioned to make a Nubian, and who had had a breakthrough here at the conference and was going to have another go at it.

Amy felt good about what they'd accomplished. It was a lot of work, but she'd flown in a biplane and she'd gotten the word out about the message in the sky. There would be another conference next year and while she was sure she could get Jim to go, she didn't think they'd get the opportunity to talk. There were experiencers who'd been abducted every other week, experiencers with alien mentors who'd practically raised them. They had so much more to say and they had new information every year. There were ex-military who could tell the same stories over and over. And there were channelers, like Christie Lewis, who had instant access to beings light years away. Amy felt lucky to have shared the stage with them, and to have been lifted out of her middling routines to share something important. The Vulcan mind melds tasted better and she found herself humming along to "Fly Like an Eagle" on the jukebox.

She didn't know Cher had been having out of body experiences through meditation, and she could contact entities who could keep her presenting at the Ozarks Conference for years. Next year they would send a camera crew and Amy would be furious when she'd learn on Cher's blog how she'd been accepted to give another talk. A few weeks later, a professionally produced YouTube video where Cher explained that she'd started meditating shortly after a UFO appeared to her and she'd been writing the answers to questions sent to her from all over the world, which would be a book from Christie Lewis's publisher. Amy never saw meditation as an avenue for revenue and Cher's success in this would drive Amy insane with jealousy. Amy had told her story about the message in the sky and it was a dead end. She still didn't know what they'd been trying to tell her, so there wasn't enough for a second conference presentation and there certainly wasn't enough for a book. Jim would happen upon her as she watched Cher's video and when Amy explained what it was, he said, "That's cool." But it was not cool. When Cher talked about the UFO she made it sound like she was the only one out there in her backyard. And when Cher talked about "my friend" Christie Lewis there was no mention of Amy who had contacted Christie in the first place. This book of hers was going to be a scam, a bunch of predictably dumb questions and vague answers. There was no way the E.T.s had chosen Cherise Trump as their ambassador.

"She's making it up!" Amy said.

"You don't know that," Jim would say. But this was the wrong thing to say. Because Amy had been upset with the universe for rewarding the ridiculous people next door, and Jim had reminded her of her anger.

"Cher's full of shit!" Amy said. "How can you take her side?"

"I didn't know there were sides," Jim would say, and: "Don't you want to go this year?"

"No I don't want to go this year."

"Me neither," Jim would tell her. And this was true. He'd been trying to figure out a way to talk Amy out of going again for his own reasons, because he was scared to death of what he might do if he found himself alone with another emotionally vulnerable woman. And between this last day of the conference and this day several months in the future where he'd run into Amy watching Cher's professionally produced Ozarks YouTube video, he'd rack his brain trying to think of a good excuse for why he and Amy shouldn't return.

Christie Lewis had covered half of her hotel room with plastic drop cloths where she'd set up a table with a block of clay and the Nubian sat facing her at the end of the bed.

She said, "You know what I'm afraid of?"

"I do."

"That I don't have the skill to render you."

"Don't look here," he said as he pointed at his face. "Look here," and he tapped the center of his temple.

She didn't know if he meant that she should look *with* her third eye, or if she should look into *his* third eye, but she hoped to do both, and whether the sculpture was any better because of it, she couldn't say, but at least she was more relaxed, less hesitant, and open to fucking it up, because it wouldn't be her that was wrong but the complainer, with everybody an art critic these days. She smoothed out the clay and duplicated his features, including and especially the tall Afro and his necklace with the pendant. She worked fearlessly, without negativity and he spoke encouraging words into her mind.

"You are good and you are good at this. People will be glad."

She wet her hands and shaped the head. She slapped handfuls of clay on top to stack up into a 'fro, and she smoothed it together.

"You went to my friend's talk," Christie said. "What do you know about the symbols in the sky?"

"When they come," the Nubian said, "when they are seen, your understanding of things changes. They left their mark."

"It's about being seen?" Christie said.

"To affect changes."

"Positive, negative, or neutral?"

"They don't really control the changes," he said. "That depends on our perception."

"Or who they are?"

"And who we are."

"They put inkblots in the sky and it changes us?"

"Of course."

"This sounds in tune with what the Zetas are telling me."

"Before you knew about the symbols," he said, "You might have been talking to Thetas, or Betas."

"Wait, *what*?"

"You can't know what has changed, because you live in the now, but change has rippled through humanity."

"Is it dangerous for them to mimic the symbols with skywriting?"

"If the skywriting creates a curiosity that leads back to knowledge of the event, then change will accelerate. Is this dangerous? Different is different. It's not always worse or better."

Christie wanted to photograph the Nubian, to capture his features and his skin tone, but she knew this wouldn't be allowed. Could a photograph affect change in the same way? It would drive her crazy if she thought too much about it, wondering what was lost and who she'd once been. Maybe she'd had the talent to sculpt a dignified and realistic Nubian. Maybe she'd changed so many times she only vaguely resembled herself anymore.

"If I put sculptures out into the world, do they also cause change, if they refer back to these events?"

"You shouldn't stop making them. And you shouldn't be afraid."

When the Nubian was gone, and she had slept on it, her doubts crept back. It was time to leave and she had to pack up the new bust to take home and she was staring back at what looked like a caricatured black man. She knew she couldn't take money from Cher and she knew she was going to have to keep the sculpture, without posting it on her website and without adding a glaze. He would remain a terra cotta

Nubian and he would remind her of their encounter, but she couldn't let it go beyond that, despite his encouraging words, because she lived at a time when white people delighted at calling each other racist. Sooner or later, one of them would find this thing she'd made while channeling and they'd question everything she'd done and everything she'd said, because there was no way a person of that type would accept her sculpture of the Nubian with an open mind or an open heart, and they'd post the image to Twitter hoping to belittle her life's work so that something they Tweeted might go viral. She would have to tell Cher that yes, she'd met the Nubian, and he'd done as she'd suggested: he'd posed for her, graciously and kindheartedly. But it wasn't enough and there was no way she was going to be able to show her the results, because the world wasn't ready for that.

We didn't deserve half of what we'd gotten. We'd catapulted out of the twentieth century and used the pinnacle of technology not for connectedness, but for snark. Out of the intentions of rising above sexism and racism we were now ruled over by the smartest kids in the class. They were self-centered jerks. They rode in Ubers like it was their birthright. They took pictures of expensive meals and sent them out for strangers to envy. They flew to distant cities to weekend in trendy bars. They wore colorful new clothes and sent out pictures of their expensive shoes too. And these experts on sexism and racism were always ready to tear others down.

"I can't even show it to you," Christie told Cher over the phone.

"It's that bad?"

"*We're* that bad. He's actually pretty good."

Arnie Fishman was at the hangar early, with the sun below the horizon, the sky pink. The bay was open, his prop where he'd parked it, but someone stood between himself and the plane, a man in sunglasses who had come to their talk. A white Lincoln with tinted windows idled on the tarmac.

Arnie extended a hand to strike up a conversation but the man wasn't interested in being friendly.

He said, "I need you to tell me you aren't going to pull any more stunts like that."

Arnie made a decent living from crop dusting, and he loved to fly. He didn't go seeking UFOs, but they had come to him, first through Amy, then he'd had his own sighting.

"Can you tell me something?" Arnie said.

"Shoot."

"What does all of this mean? Who are they? Where do they come from? What do they want?"

The man moved his lips around like he'd had a wad of gum he'd forgotten about but that Arnie had reminded him of.

"You want to know?"

"I'm curious."

"Supposing I did know, which I don't, why would I tell you?"

"I'm part of it now," Arnie said. "And I should maybe know why."

The man took a deep breath and he let it out.

"Of all the things you might want to know, that's the one?"

"I'll take it to my grave."

The man took off his glasses to reveal the yellowy whites of a drinker. He looked like he hadn't slept. He had gray streaks in his unwashed hair and gray in his beard stubble.

"They're from out there. But so are we. They've been charged with maintaining the garden. And so have we. Our stories are intertwined. We don't know how we began or how it will end. They, however, see everything at once."

"Like fate?"

"We can change it. We have changed it. And that's why you need to stop doing what you've been doing."

"It's really a message?"

"I don't know."

"It makes the UFO-nuts happy," Arnie said. "They loved seeing it."

"They just want to be a part of something. This feels big to them."

"Is it big?"

"It's big."

"So what else do they get?" Arnie said. "What else can they be a part of that's big?"

"We can't exactly stop them. They're going to talk to each other on the Internet. They're going to keep looking to the skies. They're going to dig in to ancient history. And they're going to meditate and walk the astral plane."

"But no more skywriting?"

"I think it's best. They might like it too much. It's too immediate. Too real."

"Some of them have had contact. Isn't that immediate and real?"

The Major put his sunglasses back on as a way of bringing the conversation to a close. He'd said what he needed to, and he felt the pilot understood.

"Their experiences are dreamy. Even in broad daylight. As much as they believe, they have doubts."

"You want them to doubt?"

The Major walked back to the white Lincoln and he opened the door on the back passenger's side, where Arnie saw uniformed guards.

"I don't call the shots," he said. "I do what I'm told."

here was a line to check out of the conference hotel, with Jim, Amy, Cher, and Tommy all standing with their bags as Christie came down the hall with a valet who pulled a cart loaded with stacked cardboard boxes. Cher knew that in the boxes were the busts she didn't sell, most likely the Reptilians and Insectoids who weren't as popular as the Grays, with their oval heads and almond-shaped black eyes, the familiar E.T.s celebrated in pop culture. The lesson at Ozarks was that anything with a Gray on it sold well.

Cher waved her over and as Christie and Cher stood there talking, Amy became concerned that to everyone else it looked like they'd helped Christie Lewis cut the line. What would the Zetas say about that?

Cher said, "Please let me have it. I want it."

But Christie shook her head and Cher could hardly believe that the alien she most desired was right there in one of those boxes, because she'd commissioned Christie, and she wasn't going to be able to have it.

Also in the line was the Major, who despite his above-top-secret security clearance had to check out like everyone else.

As was Val, the Lyft driver, who fidgeted because she really needed to get on the road. She'd packed light so she could pick up passengers for the long haul home, and it seemed all these believers and experiencers, with their bags loaded down with t-shirts, ball caps, refrigerator magnets, and other souvenirs, were checking out much too slowly. As the people in the back of the line glared at Christie Lewis, who really had cut, she demonstrated a practiced ability to completely ignore the negative energy that was directed toward her, and Val noticed Jim standing with Amy. Val looked down at her yellow Converse high-tops that she'd restrung with pink shoelaces as she felt her heart being pulled in that direction. That was the guy. He wasn't even going to come over and say anything to her and she might never see him again. She knew Dr. Z would be able to contact him but also knew he happened to be one of those ethical therapists who would be unlikely to give her his number no matter how desperate she became. And as much as Cher wanted to open all of Christie's cardboard boxes like it was Christmas, Val wanted to go say something to Jim. Until eventually she did.

She realized she'd be giving up her place in line by walking up to them, and the later she got started, the demand for riders would go down, but she wanted Jim to know that she was here in this line and it wasn't okay for him to ignore her like that.

"I want to tell you I'm a fan of your work," Val said to Christie, "but it's awkward because these people are angry with you because you cut the line."

"I didn't cut," Christie said loudly enough for the people in line to hear. "I had my friends hold my place because I had to make sure the valet had all the right boxes."

Christie said it like she was a hypnotist and Val was supposed to accept what she said because of the manner in which she'd said it. But Val had been hypnotized plenty of times and she knew that wasn't how it worked. She suspected that Christie looked down on Val, because Val would never have half the things Christie had: a place that she owned, a talent for the arts, a business, respect from the UFO community, and an ongoing mutually beneficial connection to a race of space aliens who had singled her out as one of the few Earth humans they kept an open line with.

Val looked down at Jim's shoes, afraid to look him straight in the face, out of fear that she was blushing, and he was in the same Florsheims he'd worn in her hotel room. He didn't even take them off. Then she did look him in the face, and he looked caught. He was afraid that she would give him away and while she wanted to, she knew it was the wrong move. If she ever wanted to be able to contact him, she had to play it cool. He was a married guy. She knew that now.

Christie stood her ground and Amy looked at Val suspiciously, because she stood there too long and to the people in line it might look like she was trying to cut as well. But Val wanted something more and she didn't want to give up.

"Who are you, again?" Amy said, and she was suggesting that Christie Lewis was Ozark Conference royalty and if she wanted to cut the line everyone should just be okay with it, because here was the ambassador of the Zetas, whom they should respect.

"I'm not anybody," Val said, and she walked back to her place at the end of the line.

"Who was that?" Amy said to Jim because she noticed the way he'd been watching her.

"She's an experiencer," Jim said. "A real one."

"How do you know?" Christie said. "They might do to her like they've done you."

"I thought you didn't believe in any real ones," Amy said.

"I think I do now," Jim said.

"Really?" Amy said. She was so excited she sprung up and made a small hop. "You believe?"

"I don't know what it is," Jim said. "We may never know what it is. But something is going on."

Hotel sex, Amy thought to herself. She had cured her husband of his stubbornness, and of his anxieties, with hotel sex. When he was bottled up again, she would know just what to do.

Part III

In his bed late at night with the curtains drawn, Ranger Nelson lay awake as lights danced above the wild forest. He hadn't grown completely apathetic in recent years, but when a loan hiker submitted a request to stay in one of the primitive sites deep in the park, the ranger tried to steer the guy closer to where the RVs were, or closer to the highway, without making it seem like that's what he was doing. And most of them were fine. Most of the time they came back out like it was nothing. But on a night like this, with an eerie sense that they were being visited, the ranger knew he'd check the hiking log in the morning, read the name and remember the face, sure that another had gone missing well before he tramped out to the deserted site.

He'd stopped asking the families to put in requests at all the agencies. He'd stopped bringing in cub reporters from the local stations to tell them the things they might air once, but never again. He couldn't even really bring it up with the other park employees, because there was too much turnover, and he was never sure who might have been hired to watch him. If someone disappeared it was just something that happened out here, and trying to fix this only made things worse. There were ghost stories supposedly handed down from the Native Americans. From the descriptions of the phenomena, Ranger Nelson had come to the conclusion that there was a portal out there. And late at night, when the stars were aligned and the conditions were right, this portal opened so that one might walk through it to another world, or one might be visited, or a craft might come through to pluck people like wildflowers, and to carry them to wherever the portal connected, where they might never return.

Though they sometimes did return. Years later. It was rare but it had happened, and since there was no official missing persons report and no ongoing news story, Ranger Nelson would go back through the logs, and he'd find where they'd signed in, and then he'd be able to look in his files for a contact. He'd drive them to the diner in Bell Trace, buy them the blue plate special, a room in the motel down the road, and enough quarters to call the number that he'd written down on a slip of paper: a wife, or a brother, or a mother. And then he wouldn't hear from them again. Understandably, they didn't want to return to the park. So he had the ride out to the diner with them and maybe forty-five minutes while they ate to probe them for answers, at least as much as they remembered, about where they'd been, how they'd gotten there, and how they'd stayed alive all that time.

The key word was time. What it was versus how it seemed. They'd walked into a mist or they'd walked into a light, or they'd been zapped up through the roof of their tent, examined with dark unblinking eyes, and spun out into the black depths of the sky. They were hungry, but rested, and in the same clothes, though the buttons were mismatched, or the shirt might be inside out. And their hair, or their beards hadn't grown any longer. They'd been gone what felt like a few days, with no way of accounting for lost time. Anxious from everything that buzzed around them over the course of their meal in this typical small-town diner, with the TV on sports and the truckers smoking and laughing at some joke, these truckers with no idea how close they'd come to one who'd gone missing but had come back, with no explanation, and no expectation to ever be able to talk about it with anyone, other than this ranger, who really truly believed them.

Tomorrow he'd check the log and walk the campsites and if someone had gone missing, he'd hope that as bizarre as it was and as unspeakable for everyone involved, that they'd also return in this way some years down the road, and that was why he couldn't quit, or ask to be moved to another park. Because he knew what he knew and he was the one to shepherd them back into their lives, as rare as it was, as unnervingly miraculous as it was when they sometimes returned wide-eyed, whole, and alive.

ack home, Jim Clinton had the feeling that someone had been in the house. He couldn't prove it. He couldn't point to anything out of place. But he knew that whoever had been taking him must have known they were gone. He didn't know what they'd hope to find, but didn't really know what they wanted from him in the first place. Amy was tired from the flight, and he was too, but he was too anxious to go to bed.

"You know what?" he said. "I've got work to catch up on. The conference was fun and all but I've got some things to do."

He wasn't really lying. He was supposed to be working remotely for two of the days while they were gone, but he also wasn't going to get anything done tonight. He was paralyzed by the idea that as soon as he fell asleep they would come in through the back door and smuggle him into the alley. He didn't know which was worse, really being abducted or being fake-abducted. Because the point of a fake abduction was to intimidate him and to make him believe things that weren't really true. Though the point of a real abduction, if he was to believe what Dr. Z had told everyone, was to steal his genes. And as much as that bothered him, he wasn't even sure his genes were his. There were thousands, no, probably millions of years of humans before him who contributed to his being Jim. Yet, he had an obligation to offspring. He wouldn't have wanted to be born some kind of hybrid freak, and he didn't want his sons and daughters to be hybrids either. So he had helped that woman, what was her name? Things would become too complicated too easily if he contacted her. He was sure Amy would leave him. He loved Amy. He loved their life together. Even with her UFO obsession and her tendency to be too kind to that asshole, Tommy Trump.

At his laptop, at the kitchen table, as Amy slept, he browsed Dr. Z's website as a way of trying to jog his memory about the woman at the conference, the abductee, but there was nothing. He had the sensation that someone stood behind him, but when he turned there was no one there.

Airman Riley sat double-lotus on a wrestling mat in an Air Force dojo as the Major paced in front of him and Riley read over Jim Clinton's shoulder.

"He's reading about regression therapy for abductees."

"Good," said the Major. "He's a believer?"

"Appears to be. I don't think he sees me, but he knows I'm here."

"Whisper in his ear."

"Why would I do that?"

"To fuck with him, I don't know."

"Why this guy?"

"He's the key. They wrote him a message and he's spreading it across the globe. We need to get him good and confused. We need him to go away or take it back."

"I don't really feel comfortable with this. Can't you just hack his website or something?"

"Not our department. We hack minds."

"You're going to have to get someone else," Riley said.

"You can't say 'no' to me. You're being paid."

"I'm not the guy for this. If I abuse it, I lose it."

"Okay, okay," the Major said. "But can you get me his passwords?"

"I'll watch," Riley said, "but I think we're wasting time."

In the middle of her bed, Cher sat cross-legged wearing her favorite yoga pants, her laptop in front of her, open to Christie Lewis's web page. She meditated on Christie's address and in her mind she walked down the street and through the door. Christie Lewis faced her, surrounded by her famous heads, including the one Cher wanted, her African. She commissioned the work and brought artist and subject together. It should be hers. She should be able to buy it.

With her eyes closed Christie Lewis said, "I know you're here," and "I don't have anything for you."

"Please?"

"Sorry."

"What do the Zetas say?"

"About the head?"

"Will you ask?"

"They don't care. They leave us to our devices."

"But you don't want to give him to me?"

"Look at him," she said. "He's awful."

"I don't see that," Cher said. "I see a noble visitor. An emissary."

"I've been doing this a long time," Christie said. "People want Grays with big black almond-shaped eyes. They want angelic blue Avians. They even want soul-crushing reptilians. You're the only one who wants a Nubian."

"Because he's real. We saw him!"

"None of this is real."

"It's a con?"

"It's a business."

"But your business is to get the truth out."

"I'm not interested," Christie said. "This is bigger than you know. You shouldn't play around outside your body."

"Is it dangerous?"

"Why ask me? You should've found out beforehand."

"So is it dangerous?"

"Isn't it obvious? What if you get lost? What do you hope to find?"

"I don't know. I still don't know. I just wanted him was all."

"I'm sorry, but he's not for sale. Now go. Get on. Please leave."

ommy Trump sat across from Cher in the breakfast nook. He wasn't dressed for work but she was afraid to ask. He'd been through some changes and she worried he'd done something drastic.

"You feeling okay?"

"They found out. Everybody knows."

"Who found what out?" Cherise thought maybe someone saw him moonlighting at Little Patriots Daycare, but how could they complain about that? It was public service and really cute. He wore funny hats and played with the kids.

"They found out about the conference. I had a new client and he Googled me, which they do, because they want to know who they're dealing with. And there was my name on the program, giving a talk about a UFO experience, and the people who were there blogged about us, with pictures of us and everything."

"So?"

"So I lost the account."

"Isn't that discrimination?"

"Rich says he wants me to take some time off. To let my head settle."

"He said that? About your head? What did you say?"

"I said these things are real, Rich."

"He wasn't open to that?"

"He was *not* open to that."

"You're taking time off?"

"It escalated. But it's not all bad. I've been thinking of a new career."

"You could still be in sales. Sell something else."

"I don't want to sell," Tommy said. "I think I want to teach."

"You hated school."

"I could do some good. I could cut through the lies."

"You'd talk about UFOs? To schoolchildren?"

"Someone has to."

"How are you going to work that in? In geometry class? In choir? What could you even teach?"

"It doesn't matter. It's easy, right? The answers are in the teacher's edition."

"You have to be certified. You can't just apply."

"But they need teachers."

"Take a few days and talk to Rich. You're not shaping any futures, but you make good money and we need it."

"There's got to be something else."

"If we moved to Chicago," Cher said. "But then we'd have to live an hour from the city, or in an overpriced condo."

"I don't want to move to Chicago."

"Then apologize to Rich."

"Am I going to lie and say it was all a big mistake?" Tommy said.

"Maybe it was."

"You saw it too. That thing was real. You've been meditating. You bought clay heads."

"We know what we know, but it's not our job to change anyone's mind. They'll never believe until they see for themselves."

"We can't keep it to ourselves."

"We live in Nappanee. We need your job. No one will believe us anyway."

"It was just one vendor. I can go back. I can still work sales."

Amy was at her laptop sending thank-you emails. She sat at the kitchen table looking out into the backyard where it all began. She thanked everyone she met who worked for the conference, and she thanked all the conference attendees who encouraged her. They loved talking to a recent convert, many with good advice. There was a surprising number of them with business cards and websites. She learned very quickly the new thing was podcasts and YouTube channels. They could talk for an hour with anyone about UFOs and many of them did, often twice a week. Here she was worried about updating her blog with new photos and insights and all she had to do was turn on a mic and talk. Somewhere down the road, maybe in two years, she'd let the website die. She'd chronicled their experience and had run out of new things to say. Maybe Cher was the smart one, for keeping a blog, because a blog was like a diary where the subject was yourself. Not solving some big mystery but whatever was going on in your life. Cher didn't have to learn anything about UFOs. She could simply write about herself.

After the last email Amy opened a blank document ready to start a new blog. But the white page on the screen was intimidating. She knew what to say to strangers when she was in a thankful mood, but talking to herself about herself, that was a new one. What could she say that wouldn't be upsetting to Jim? Because that was mostly where her head was these days. What had been wrong with him and what could she do about it? They couldn't exactly go back to living like they had before, because they'd been shown something huge. And she didn't know how to manifest the changes in a positive way. She didn't want to go back to school, or to get a job, or to volunteer anywhere. She didn't want a dog or a cat, or a kid. She would be kinder, she would be more appreciative, and she would leave larger tips. These would be incremental changes that no one else would know about, but they would make a difference to her. She shut the laptop, but she resolved to find something to say. She could start by writing a big generic thank you to the universe for having put her in the path of the UFO, and therefore of the conference, where everyone was terrific. Amy didn't even know she'd had a community, but she'd found them last week. They were smart, optimistic, and open to anything. And she wanted to be more like them.

She opened the laptop again and she typed. She remembered going to church as a child and feeling smarter than everyone. How could all those adults believe in what seemed a children's story? But what she knew now was that wanting to believe wasn't the same as believing, and most of the time it was good enough. It was what was so frustrating about Jim, though she left that part out. He didn't even want to believe. He was so sure that he didn't. And that's what she hated about the most vocal churchgoers, their certainty, and what she hoped for most for her own spiritually was *possibility*. Not to live forever, or to see God. But the *possibility* of something else, whatever that might be. And she knew that possibility was what they'd all seen in the backyard that day. Was it real? Possibly. Did it matter? Probably. Was it speaking to them? Maybe. Would she try to contact them or talk to them? She didn't know. And she was okay with not knowing. Was she afraid of them? Sometimes. Did she know where she was heading with her brand new blog? Not at all. Was she excited about it? Kind of.

In a dojo on a military base, Airman Riley sat lotus-style in Air Force issue shorts and a t-shirt as his superior paced in front of him barefoot but otherwise in full dress uniform on the squishy wrestling mat. Riley had been told to travel to another base, where a thirty-foot saucer was parked in a hangar. It was covered with a tarp but was a perfect circle and it also levitated, so there was no reason to cover it, no confusion about what was under the tarp.

"I need you to walk around the innards. Can you make a blueprint?"

"I cannot," he said. "Aren't there other ways of reverse-engineering?"

"We can't cut it apart. There are no screws or rivets. It's one big piece."

"An organic whole," Riley said. "Which is why I can't get inside. It would be like walking around in you. Your soul wouldn't allow it."

"It has a soul?" The Major said and he stopped in his tracks.

"It has something. We may as well call it a soul."

The Major became agitated and he paced again as he tried to think of a workaround.

"How is it," he said, "that we can shoot these things down, but can't look inside one of them?"

"How do you shoot them down?"

"They react to radar. It messes with them somehow, and they crash."

"It's because they're being seen," Riley said. "Radar shows them when they don't want to be seen, when they're not supposed to be seen, and that affects space-time."

"Seeing it?"

With his eyes still closed, Riley nodded.

"With the radar?"

He nodded again.

"If we don't get results," he said, "We get taken off this project."

"I'm doing what you want," Riley said. "But there are limits.

Riley opened his eyes and said, "Let me ask you something."

"Shoot."

"You've got saucers?"

"We do."

"And you can fly them?"

"Kind of."

"Kind of?"

"The seats are small. There's not a lot of headroom. The control mechanism wants a sixth finger."

"But you can fly it? Someone short can fly it?"

"Yes."

"Then what else do you want?"

"It's not good enough. We have excellent reconnaissance planes. We don't need another one."

"You want to put a missile on it?"

"Precisely."

"You're not going to be able to do that."

"And why not."

"It's perfectly symmetrical. The only reason it can do what it does, is because it's perfectly symmetrical."

"We have symmetrical missiles."

"It's not going to work."

"Then how do they?..."

"Make war? They don't."

"But how do we?..."

"We don't."

"Listen, Airman," The Major said. "Weapons is what we do. It's our purpose."

"Let me talk to the pilots."

"They died," the Major said. "It's what happens when you shoot them down."

"To the ship, then."

"You can talk to the ship?"

"I think so. It's not going to understand the concept of a missile, however."

"How about an energy weapon? A laser, or microwaves or something?"

"It can direct energy, but only if it wants to."

"You asked it already?"

"It's something I know."

"Ask it."

"It won't like being asked what I already know."

"It knows what you know?"

"If I'm going to communicate with it, there's a connection between us."

"What about a bomb? Not necessarily nuclear, but like a Daisycutter or something?"

"I'm not going to ask it about a bomb."

"Just try. For me?"

"It may refuse to talk to me afterwards."

"This flying machine has scruples?"

"More than you, sir. For sure."

"I am protecting our country. You remember that. We don't know where these green guys came from."

"We do."

"Or what they're up to."

"I can ask."

"They're not very good invaders. It must be something else. Something sneaky."

"I can ask."

"Yes," the Major said and he nodded in appreciation of this new tactic. "Talk to this ship and find out what they're up to."

"Can we go there?"

"Go where?"

"To the ship. It's in a hangar, right?"

"That's need to know."

"It might respond better if I'm there."

"Let me send a message up the chain."

"Thank you, sir," Riley said. "I feel good about this."

After two years of driving, Val had come to the conclusion that the Lyft app was garbage. She looped around downtown South Bend for an hour without a single ride, and when she finally got a ping nineteen minutes away it took her south into Amish country. Of course the rider canceled before she could arrive and she was vulnerable on the country roads where she was alone. Time slowed as she sped through cornfields and dust motes drifted through sunlight in her car. She got a ping that sent her down a dirt road, which would nullify the car wash she'd gotten yesterday, though no one ever complained about the condition of her car, and she'd even been abducted while she had a passenger in the back without Lyft deactivating her account. People wanted rides. People wanted you to take them to the airport or to drive them home from the bars. She wished more of them knew how little she made, because they always wanted to talk about money: was she busy, had she had a lucrative day?

In the bright blue sky was a triangular-shaped cloud that could only be artificial and she was sure she was about to be taken. She looked in her rearview to see if there were any cars behind her, because it was safer to pull over and wait. But she saw someone sitting in her backseat. He had long hair and a beard and she glanced over at her phone on the dash mount to see his name, Philip. She didn't remember picking him up or where they were going, but she continued in the direction indicated by the navigational map. She would have made small talk but didn't know if she already had. She was in the middle of some kind of episode but didn't want to appear out of sorts to the passenger.

"Look at that!" he said, and she knew by the way he said it, there was one in the sky.

It was a saucer four car-lengths wide and it dipped down to get a look at her.

"Have you ever seen one?" she said, but he appeared to be frozen, like a mime in timeout. He didn't even breathe.

A blinding green light came out of the craft and she slowed and averted her eyes as she tried to concentrate on the road. Lights moved over the surfaces inside her car and she sensed them peering into her as well, at her flowing veins, her guts, and her thoughts. She was terrified. She pulled over and locked the doors.

"They'll probably leave you here," she said. "You'll wake up with me gone and will have to hail another ride. I'm sorry but there's really nothing I can do."

The ship descended so it was nearly on top of them, with her hair standing up from the electric field, the hum of high voltage in her head, flashes behind her shut eyelids, and she shouted "Please stop!"

They were so close she sensed there were three of them in the ship. She had a vision of the future where she held an at-home pregnancy test as the lines materialized and it confirmed what she knew. She saw herself in a job where she sat at a desk and she wore a skirt and a blouse with a jacket. When she woke up from her visions, the saucer lifted up and shot away.

She got out of the car and walked around it for signs of what she'd witnessed, with the smell of ozone in the air. There was someone in the backseat, sitting up but asleep. And when she touched the door handle to get back in, she was shocked with a static discharge that made her yelp. To which the passenger responded, "Where are we?"

"We hit a pothole," Val said. "I was checking the tires."

"I didn't notice."

"What's the last thing you remember?"

"I must have dozed off."

When Val was driving again, she felt joy bubble up inside her when she realized she was free. She'd been in the dumps over that man at the conference, but now she didn't care about him. Because her future was hers. They would leave her alone now. Maybe for good. If she'd gotten here from a stupid transgression that was so unlike her, and among the dumbest things she'd ever done, though merely a misdemeanor on her soul ledger, then it was absolutely worth it for what she'd gained.

She didn't have to go driving at night. She could wait tables again, for more money, or she'd apply for that clerk job at the sheriff's office, where she'd get benefits and time off. She knew some of the guys down there because she'd driven them, and also been pulled over by them. When they asked if she knew she was driving over the speed limit, she said, "I've been out here driving drunks all night, and I just wanted to get home," which they appreciated, and so they let her go. For the first time in a long time, Val had the feeling that everything would be okay.

Tommy Trump was early for his shift at Little Patriots Daycare. His boss was the daughter of the woman who owned the place, half his age and not much of a manager. He never fit in with the women who worked there, and when he apologized for quitting, she said, "Everyone quits sooner or later."

"I think I want to go into teaching," Tommy said. "With older kids. Do you know any schools that are hiring?"

His boss said, "Mostly, they hire the student-teachers."

"How do you get that?"

"You go to college."

"I already went to college."

"You go back. There are tests and things."

"Over what?"

"It depends what you want to teach."

"I want to be a role model," Tommy said. "I want to tell them what's going on."

"What do you think is going on?"

Tommy sized up the young woman and knew not to trust her.

"I don't know," he said. "I guess I want summers off."

Just then Tommy saw his adversary, the weird little kid, Roger, being dropped off by his mother who stared straight ahead and drove off without acknowledging anyone around her. Roger had wanted Tommy gone and Roger smiled as he walked by like he knew everything that had been said.

"You could teach Dumbology," Roger said, and it was a mean joke that should have been beyond a kid so young, but they'd gotten used to the strange things Roger said, and Tommy realized he'd given Roger just what he wanted. No one would be there to counter his tyranny with the princesses, and none of the other daycare workers had the will to push back. Little Patriots was Roger's daycare now. And as much as Tommy hated to betray the kids, he couldn't stay any longer. His head was filled with his recent experiences at the Ozarks Conference, and it was time to go.

"Catch you on the flipside, Roger."

The kid was puzzled by that, and Tommy knew he'd be turning over the phrase in his weird little brain for weeks.

Dr. Z was in shadow and his silhouette took up half the computer monitor. He told Val to watch the glowing ball on the wall behind him, which cycled through deep tints of orange, indigo, rose, and violet. Val relaxed enough to surrender her will, so she would know and remember.

"Think back to the last time," he said. "The most recent incident."

"I was in a hotel room."

"At the Ozarks?" he said. "They came for you there?" Then he added, "I guess I shouldn't be surprised."

"He took off my robe. I hadn't been with anyone in a long time, and I let him."

"You're not talking about Grays?"

"I was awake. I was aware. I remember."

"This sounds personal," Dr. Z said. " We don't have to talk about it."

"I want to. Because you know him. You regressed him."

"I see."

"*You* brought us together."

"Like fate?"

"I don't know. I think I'm pregnant."

"It's too soon. You can't know."

"I know."

"Have they told you this?"

"They came and they left."

"Has that ever…"

"No."

"So this is good?"

"It won't be easy, but it's good. I think it will be good."

"A relief?"

"Yes."

"And they won't come back?"

"It's what they wanted from me, and now they can't have me. So they're gone."

"Do you wish to continue?" Dr. Z said.

"With regressions?"

"With any of this?"

"I'd like to keep talking," Val said. "I know it's not how this is supposed to work, but you might be my only friend."

In the elevator of the Ruth Withersby Business and Mass Communications Building, Tommy wore one of the many suits from his closet, so he didn't look like a student, and he didn't look quite like a professor. On the fourth floor, the elevator opened and he stepped past a kid in a pair of red and blue sweats with the screaming eagle on his chest, the kid bigger than Tommy, a SpongeBob backpack slung loosely across a shoulder. Tommy had an appointment with the Dean of Business and it sounded like she was ready to hire him on the spot. After what his boss had told him at Little Patriots, he expected the process to be more rigorous and selective, but he soon understood they would hire him to teach one class, without paying benefits, and he would make less than what would cover his lunches and gas.

The secretary got up when he entered the office, and she led him to the Dean's door. "She's been expecting you."

The Dean was on the phone and she held up a finger but indicated that he should sit down. She dug through the clutter of paper and folders until she produced his application as she finished up her phone call with, "That will be splendid. I agree." And she hung up and gave Tommy her full attention.

"Can you start next week?" she said.

"So soon?"

"We've had a sudden vacancy and the semester starts a week from Monday. Gina will get you the textbook and find you a desk in the adjunct office. You'll have to share but you're only here twice a week, so it should do. How was the commute?"

"I'll have to see what traffic is like in the morning, but it was fine. It'll be fine."

"Have you ever taught sales?"

"To salesmen."

"Perfect. They'll want role-play. Maybe give them a big project. Tell them what it's like in the real world."

"That's it?"

"We're giving them a *practical* education."

"I can give it to them straight?"

"It's why you've been hired."

"No bullshit? No lies?"

"The straight dope."

"Thank you for this opportunity."

"I'm sorry we can't pay you more," she said. "But parking is free and you can use the rec. center."

Emboldened by Christie Lewis, Cher sat with her laptop in the middle of the bed. This was usually where she meditated, but today she was going to write. Christie told her she had a gift and if she sent a sample, she thought her publisher would offer a book contract. She typed out several questions she thought people would want the answers to. Then she meditated and waited for the universe to respond.

And later at The Old Mill, their go-to restaurant for celebrations, she ordered a nice bottle and toasted her husband, the college professor. For all that Tommy was, there was so much that he was not, and a college professor had always been one of the things he was never going to be. But now he was, and Cher was going to have a book. She didn't know for sure yet, but she felt it, in the same way she felt she could meditate and know the answers to everything, at least everything that could be asked, and when she told Tommy this, he asked the most obvious question, the one she didn't think to ask yet.

"What did it say?"

"What did what say?"

"The message. In your picture of the UFO."

"Oh." Cher said. She pushed her chair back and closed her eyes, but she could hear the sounds of knives and forks, the murmurs of conversation, the crackling of the burning logs in the fireplace. She tried to let go but couldn't go to that other place while she sat at a table at The Old Mill. She sipped from her wineglass and the saliva glands in her jaw stung. She knew good wine shouldn't do that, but she'd brushed her teeth before they came out and she supposed that had something to do with it. She waited but no answer came. It was like shaking the magic eight ball and seeing the message float up to the round plastic window to reveal, "Sorry, try again."

"Are you asking now?" Tommy said.

"Shush."

She loosened from herself and floated from table to table where she didn't hear the words but experienced the emotions of each conversation. She tasted bites of steak, fish, and chicken as each chewed and she pondered the paths of these life travelers, some too easily made happy and some hovering just above a base level of sadness. She wanted to help them but didn't think they would hear her, and she also didn't think there was anything she could say that would counter the predictable trajectory of their lives. Here was a girl afraid to Bat Mitzvah. Her father tried to tally the bill for their dinner in his head as a kind of game. Her mother remembered a show on the DVR she wanted to watch. Here was a county clerk who knew the secrets of people through their handwriting. There was a man with a girl who would leave him, but not yet, not for years, or not ever, but already gone and always gone in the important ways. And so Cher couldn't think about the message, because she couldn't get through the emotional currents around her, and it would have to wait until tomorrow or the next day, when she was alone with her laptop on the bed.

"I think it says, 'This is a warning'," she said.

"A warning about what?"

"That's all I get. But it's what it says."

"That doesn't sound good."

"Tell me about the job," Cher said. "It's why we're here."

"I like it. The Dean is our kind of people."

"I didn't know we had a kind."

"Not artsy-fartsy, but *real*, you know? More street-smart than book-smart."

"Conservative?"

"As you'd expect."

"Kind of rich?"

"Kind of."

"I guess we do have a people."

"That's okay, right? It's normal. It's natural."

"Are you going to order meat?" Cher said.

"I'm thinking just sides tonight."

"You're going to celebrate with *sides*?"

"I can if I want."

In bed, Amy typed on her laptop while wearing noise-cancelling headphones and Jim stared at the TV, which was off. She'd gotten the idea to take her experience and turn it into stories. She'd already written about a couple who sees a UFO and one of them stopped eating meat, and the editors at *Amazing Astronauts*, the science-fiction magazine she'd sent it to, said they liked it, though the ending was too predictable. But if she had anything else they would read more. Which she didn't, though they'd given her reason to write more, so she decided to crank out one about a couple where one of them was abducted, and he kept denying it, but this was hard to write with him sitting next to her, and he was bored because he wanted to watch TV, but he indulged her because he thought she might give him sex afterwards, though writing took a lot of time and so far she hadn't typed anything at all.

She didn't know where to begin. She couldn't open with a UFO in the sky because that was how she'd started her first story, and the editors would remember. That would be an easy "no" for them.

She'd showered before bed and was naked under her bathrobe, in one of the hotel bathrobes from the conference. She'd liked them so much she bought a pair when they checked out, and she was glad, because she wanted to take something from that experience with her and she loved a long bath and wearing a comfy bathrobe afterwards was a good way to prolong the soothing nature of the bath and to take that feeling with her to bed.

Jim stared straight ahead at the blank TV and he slid his hand casually up and down her thigh. He was aroused and he wanted her. She decided to start with a description of him and then maybe a scene would develop from there.

She typed, "Her husband was horny again but she wasn't in the mood." That was as true a sentence as she'd ever written and she was sure the editors at *Amazing Astronauts* would like it. So she built on her story from there: "They'd been married seven years and if he was more interested in sex these past six months, he'd also been more emotionally distant, a direct result of his abductions. They would come for him, and she would be unable to move, and Jim (she knew she couldn't call him Jim in the story, but she'd fix that later)...he'd be gone for hours. When he returned he couldn't explain where he'd been. He never wanted to talk about it, which made him guarded, which she found to be a turn off, and so she denied him. She didn't know if he wanted her because it had been a while, or if there was something about the abductions that aroused him, something they'd done to him or suggested to him, that made him keen to procreate, and she was afraid of this too. Because what if they'd done something to his genes? She didn't really want a baby, and she for sure didn't want a baby that was some kind of cosmic experiment."

The typing came easily but only for a while, because Jim's slow stroking had reached the point were his fingers were in her pubic hair and she didn't want to be mean about it, but he'd forced her to shut him down.

"Did you want to watch TV?"

"Not if it will bother you."

"I've got headphones on. I can write and listen to Bach."

"Maybe I don't really want to watch TV."

"You want sex?"

"If you do."

"And what if I don't?"

"Maybe I still do."

"Can you wait? Can you wait until I'm done with this?"

"I can wait. But is that a 'yes'?"

"*Yes, but you've got to stop touching me.*"

"I can stop. But that's a 'yes'? For later?"

"Go make me some coffee," Amy said. "And you might have to wait for more than an hour."

"I can wait more than an hour."

"You might wait more than two."

"Maybe I will watch TV," he said. "But you said we could when you're done?"

"I said 'yes.'"

"And 'yes' means 'yes'?"

"I don't know, probably? Maybe?"

"What are you writing about? Is this for your blog?"

"You need to stop talking before I change my mind."

Her read over what she had so far and while it was only a few pages she thought it might be enough to send to Christie's publisher:

"Do trees think?"

"Yes, but slower. It would take an hour or more to translate what they think in real time."

"But they know we're here?"

"Yes."

"Do they like us?"

"They like children."

"Not adults?"

"Too many bad experiences."

"They're conscious?"

"Yes."

"What about after they've been turned into paper, or rowboats, or houses?"

"It depends. They might remain conscious if they were turned into something like a guitar, as long as someone was playing the guitar. But they're not conscious if they've been turned into a phone bill, or a gas station receipt. That would be too terrible. So death is a kindness. The universe has let them go blank."

"I thought all things were conscious."

"With limits."

"Like phone bills and gas station receipts?"

"If we were kinder to each other and the bills and receipts served a higher purpose, then they might be conscious too."

"So it's our fault? Our lack of awareness is harming the spiritual vibrations around us."

"I wouldn't say *harming*."

"But we have an effect? A negative effect?"

"We can. We do."

"And we can change?"

"Of course. You changed."

"I did," Cher said. "Look at me, I'm writing a book."

"Don't get an inflated ego."

"Or the book won't have consciousness?"

"That's right."

"I'm not doing it for money."

"There's no money in it."

"Or fame. So what is there besides consciousness? My book is for the greater good."

"So be it."

On his first day of school, Tommy Trump arrived early enough to be able to sit in his office and sip coffee from his Thermos before class. Instead, he circled around the campus with nowhere to park, the faculty parking pass hung from his rearview mirror, with all the faculty lots filled from the students who parked there because they knew they wouldn't be ticketed on the first day. So Tommy parked way out past the astronomy building, with its gold-domed retractable roof, and past Finley Stadium, where the band director on a cherry picker barked through a megaphone, his commands echoed among the towering brick dorms: "One more time," he said. "Let's everybody hit our marks."

Tommy walked and fought the urge to run, because being late wasn't as bad as being less late but sweating. He looked at the campus map on his phone and as he estimated the scale, he came to the conclusion that he had a mile to go and no way to make it on time. He moved briskly but realized this would also cause him to break into a sweat, so he relaxed and he imagined the things he would say as the maxim "Never be late to a meeting with a client" repeated in his head.

When he finally made it to the Ruth Withersby Business and Mass Communications Building, and he found his room, which he had thought was on the second floor, but turned out to be the big auditorium, with an entrance on the second floor where he had to come in at the top and walk past the rows of students to the front. It also took time to figure out how to log onto the computer and power up the projector screen. He looked up at the young cynical faces, and he said, "How many of you assholes are parked in the faculty lots?" and a murmur of laughter rolled around the room as a third of the students raised a hand. He had them now and he could take his time with the rest of the class, which involved taking roll, outlining the key points of the syllabus, and introducing their first assignment.

As he went down the list of names, he tried to rhyme a thing or two about each of them in his head, to remember the names, a salesman's trick. He found there were too many to be able to keep this up, so that "blonde chick with red lipstick named Melony Hemmings" worked for six or seven of them. And as he was trying to think of a rhyme for a girl in a purple Polo and khakis, he saw how she looked over at a guy in a purple Polo and khakis, who sat in the middle of a group of kids in purple Polos and khakis, and she waited for the one in the middle to nod in approval before she responded to her name being called.

"Present," she said.

When Tommy got to the guy in the middle, they all looked up as Tommy rhymed to himself, "Ringleader of the purple Polo clan named William

Williamson" and he knew this was one name he didn't have to rhyme. When he went out for dinner with Cher that night to celebrate his first day as a teacher, the name was there between them and he was thinking about him all through the meal. Will Williamson didn't have to say anything or do anything, but the other kids were drawn to him, like Roger at Little Patriots and as he was halfway through his mashed potatoes at dinner, Tommy realized the resemblance: a thinning blonde comb-over, long spindly limbs, and if you didn't look at him directly, his eyes were revealed to be large and black. He couldn't get the image of these two strange boys out of his mind and he set his fork down, unable to eat.

"Saving room for dessert?" Cher said, and Tommy couldn't muster the gumption to tell her what was going on. Here she was writing a book with all the answers to the universe and the best he could think to say to her about an alien hybrid in his class was, "I think I'm full."

Next to each other and harnessed into side-facing seats on a C-130, the Major and Airman Riley descended toward Wright-Patterson Air Force Base. Airman Riley hadn't been told where he was going and there were no windows on the cargo plane, but he closed his eyes to walk about, and was able to ascertain their destination from the pilots' conversation.

"Stop that," the Major said.

"Stop what?"

"I know you're doing it. We'll be there soon enough. I've agreed to show you a saucer. You don't have to do that."

"It's a habit and a past-time," Riley said.

After they landed, and de-planed, and jogged across the runway to the barracks, an escort walked them out to a Jeep. The escort drove, the Major sat in front, and Riley buckled himself in in the back. He was no longer surprised at how many military types never used seatbelts. They liked to be able to stand up or jump out at a moment's notice, even here on base where they weren't being shot at.

They came to a hangar with an F-22 and an F-35 parked in front with a curtain hung behind them that hid what was in the rest of the hangar. The escort led them to an armed guard who let them enter through a slit in the curtain, to where there was a B-2 and another curtain and another guard, to where there was a TR-3B, which was triangular like the B-2, and black like the B-2, but underneath there were open ports for what appeared to be engines, maybe jet engines? Maybe not? But the TR-3B was a ship that was human-made and intended for human pilots. As they went up to the last guard, and through the last curtain, they saw something so familiar and foreign that was not human-made: a sixty-foot saucer identical to the one Riley had once flown while walking about. Seeing it, he realized that as streamlined and stealthy as our most advanced aircraft were, they were made from parts, riveted together, and coated with a graphite substance, while this ship appeared to be all one perfect part. As it levitated and slowly bobbed up and down, it also pulsed brighter and gave the impression that it was alive, which Riley knew. He sat lotus at a respectful distance, until he Carol Pasternaked his way into a conversation with the thing and his consciousness moved around inside the craft from room to room.

"You don't have to do that," the Major said. "We know how to open the door. We can just go in."

And sure enough the door opened, and the Major went in as the escort waited. Riley opened his eyes, stood up, and followed behind.

There in the cockpit were chairs that were too small for them and a control panel with a six-fingered indentation.

"Go ahead," the Major said. "You know you want to."

But this was no mere indulgence. Riley knew the Major was here to learn from him, to see if he could make the saucer respond in ways others couldn't.

He placed his hand on the control and the UFO lifted to the ceiling of the hangar. Without hesitation, Riley knew they could fly through the roof without any damage to the integrity of the building, and soon they were high above Wright-Patterson, in daylight, which caused alarm, so the Major said, "You need to take us higher," and in an instant they were in space and looking down at the curve of the big blue globe wrapped with clusters of bumpy white clouds.

"Where should we go?" Riley said.

"I was hoping you knew," the Major said, though he had a list of secret sites and installations he'd had a hankering to get a look at. He just knew it was too soon. He had to get the Airman flying around first, and then he might drop the suggestion of one of these locales on him.

"I know it sounds dumb," Riley said. "But I wanted to fly over my mom's old house in Indiana."

"There's nothing dumb about that," the Major said, and the idea pleased him. He was sure that that was exactly the kind of trip that would make the Airman vulnerable to any suggestion he followed it with, and so to Indiana they went.

On the phone with Christie Lewis, Amy Clinton was reminded about the African Alien Cher blogged on and on about and she thought he might make an excellent character in a short story. But it was Christie who had called Amy. She wanted to warn Jim about his abductions.

"Some abductions are real," she said, "and some are fake."

"How does one tell?" Amy asked.

"By the dirt."

"I'm sorry?"

"With the fake ones," she said, "they originate on Earth and so they aren't as clean. There's dust and there's dirt."

"And the real ones?"

"If they've really come from space," Christie said.

"There's no dust and no dirt?"

"That's it."

"And you called to tell me this?"

"Also to let you know I have a new line of sculptures."

"I saw," Amy said, disappointed. She thought maybe a friendship was developing with Christie Lewis, or that she'd called out of genuine concern for her husband, and maybe she had, but this was also a sales call.

"They're the ant people," she said, "and I'm really excited about them."

"The ones from the Pueblo drawings?"

"Hopi," Christie said. "They saved us."

"From the blue kachina and the red kachina?"

"You know all about it," Christie said. "I don't have to tell you. It's like I'm talking to an expert."

"Trying to be."

And with that, as she browsed Christie's website, Amy was filled with the desire to buy a menagerie of ant people.

For his next class, Tommy was on time. There were more of them wearing purple Polos seated around Will Williamson, and Tommy tried to imagine their closets. Had they bought up all the purple Polos or were they washing them every day?

After an introduction to a cold-call sales technique, he told them to break into small groups, and to write call scripts.

"What are some things you could focus on?" he said. "Remember, you want to sound genuine. You want them to believe that you're presenting *an opportunity*. You can use that word, but not too much. Don't tip your hand. Don't go all in."

Some of the students moved around so they could sit next to each other, because with the auditorium seating and the way it rose up in the back, facing each other was awkward. But there was this large group in the middle, and none of them moved, and they all faced Will Williamson, who did the talking, and they each wrote down what he said: "I'm selling you very much this opportunity," he said. "This opportunity is giving you happiness."

Tommy walked up a side row to the back where he engaged with one of the small groups and he offered pointers, but the whole time he was listening to Will Williamson, who didn't get it. He was being so vague and unserious no one would ever buy anything from him. Tommy had suggested that they imagine a product: "What kind of service or device might a company try to sell with a cold call?" This had been his very first instruction. He had written it on the board, and Will had completely ignored this part of the activity. Will Williamson also ignored where he'd said "groups of three or four," and he'd written that on the board too. He felt he was being tested and he should say something, so he said, "Good job," to the group he was with, though he didn't really believe that. However, compared to what was going on with Will Willamson's group it was a very good job indeed, and he worked his way over to the perimeter of the kids in purple.

"Why don't you four form your own group?" he said, but they kept their gaze locked on Will Williamson and they continued to write down what he said.

"I'm selling you lots of things," he said. "You're wanting to buy all the things I'm selling."

And with that, Tommy broke character and he went over to the waifish kid to confront him. This took time, because he had to scooch his way through the middle aisle, until he stood before Will Williamson and he said, "What's with the purple shirts?"

This wasn't at all how he had imagined teaching would be, and he was going to have a difficult semester if this was how it had started.

Will Williamson looked at Tommy and the boy was afraid. Tommy had called attention to how he didn't fit in and it seemed this was what he had thought he had been doing, in his awkward way. He didn't like having gotten it all wrong and he couldn't change here in the middle of it all, so he continued to dictate his call-script while everyone around him wrote it down. And Will Williamson spoke louder, and soon the kids at the edges of the other groups came down to join the big group, and they were writing it down too: "You are buying this opportunity. You are in happiness when buying. You are buying all of what I am selling."

"You think this script's going to work?"

"It works."

And as he went back to the podium, Tommy understood that he didn't have to teach anything. These kids would think they were learning salesmanship and there was nothing he could tell them that they would remember. They would leave with the vague satisfaction of having gone to class and having written things down. He wasn't going to be able to fight it and he wasn't going to be able to sneak in the truth about UFOs. They were learning *a lot* about UFOs even if they weren't conscious of it. Maybe they'd never understand, but at their core they somehow knew. Maybe by circumstance they'd find themselves at Ozarks one day and the memories would come flooding back. Or maybe they'd live in service to the needs of this semi-human, without ever knowing why they did the things they did. And maybe it wasn't as bad as trying to land the big sale, or maybe it was worse, but Tommy knew he was never going to be able to just hand them the truth. People came to their own conclusions, or at least they seemed to believe so, and this was the beauty of Will Williamson's power over them: they wanted to do what he wanted them to want to do. And so, while Tommy wasn't being paid very much to teach, he also didn't have to work for it. He could come to class with his to-go coffee, write some things on the board, and surf the web while Will Williamson took over and the time filled itself. He felt slightly sorry for these kids, who were innocent victims of something they hadn't seen coming, but like the princesses at Little Patriots, he supposed they also kind of deserved it.

Amy wasn't going to wait for a response to her second story because she knew rejection was coming, so in the meantime she needed to write a new one. You wouldn't know by looking at their website, but *Amazing Astronauts* was a prestigious science-fiction magazine. Some of their writers had like ten novels, and some of them had had their stories turned into movies. There was no way those editors were going to spend more than a minute reading a story from a nobody like Amy Clinton. But once she'd learned how well published their writers were, it gave her a list of science-fiction magazines to submit to. Most of the magazines had "no simultaneous submissions" policies, which meant she could only send one story to one magazine at a time. But if she got together enough stories, which she was working toward, she could keep them in rotation until someone eventually decided they liked what she was doing. She hadn't completely figured out what she was doing, but it had to do with fictionalizing her experience as a way of getting it out there, because if people read her stories, then maybe more would believe. It sounded dumb when she thought of it like that, but she was driven. She felt like this was somehow important, like the message in the sky, even if she had no idea what it said.

At her laptop she typed, "Cornelius Heartmonger was an erotonaut from the seventh moon of Saturn, here on a mission of love."

There was no way the editors at *Amazing Astronauts* were going for this one, but she didn't care. She really liked the tone of it. She didn't have to be serious and maybe more people would read the thing and actually enjoy it.

"He was a hepcat funky player with a cosmic message to always enjoy thyself. His ride was a golden UFO with a ballroom disco dance floor, though on the outside the craft was only fifteen feet across. He was friends with William Shatner, the Dalai Lama, the Princess of Wales, and motherfucking Barack Obama. He wore a bandolier of test tubes filled with Crown Royal, he was weighted down with strings of pink pearls and gold chains, and in his blue suede buckled platform shoes he cascaded through all the moves."

Why was he here, Amy wondered? What did he want? What would happen? But the answers were so obvious she continued on in the same vein, and the narration took over. She was a writer now. All she needed was to finish this one and an editor would love it. This was something she didn't even know she wanted a few weeks ago, and it was already happening. Once her stories were out in the world she could get Jim to help her turn her website into an author's website, with a new domain: AmyClinton.com. She hadn't updated the old one since she'd been back from the conference. She supposed she should make a couple of posts about the panels as a way of wrapping up, but that felt like a chore and she was having fun now. This feeling would propel her forward in her new endeavor until she discovered Cher's book a few months down the road.

It would be the dead of winter when she saw Cher drive up Mulberry Court in their bronze Infiniti SUV, and she'd wave her down to tell her she'd had three science-fiction stories published, the news coming out of her in puffs of steam in the cold air. Three stories was enough for her to become a voting member of the Science Fiction and Fantasy Writers Association, could she believe it? She'd get to vote on the prize stories and books for the year! She could go to their conference! She'd have her name listed on their website as a member!

Then Cher told Amy about her own writing. That she'd been channeling and writing the answers down. Christie Lewis had gotten her a book deal, could she believe it? Cherise Trump would have her very own book!

And the happiness Amy had felt as a writer suddenly drained. Here was someone who didn't deserve what she'd worked so hard for, and it came too easily, like everything did for people with money. Amy wanted to scream, but all she could do, what she had to do, was to tell Cher that she was happy for her, which she wasn't, because she was incredibly jealous, and she hated being jealous, especially of Cher, because there was nothing else about Cher's life that she wanted, except this book deal, which she wanted more than anything now that she'd heard about it.

Deep in the night, at the outskirts of the Mayan ruins, where the jungle knelt before the ancient abandoned city, the locals in their hammocks were awakened by the chattering of birds and a light in the sky. They took up their bundles and they took to the paths, to the crumbling ziggurat. They kept to the cover of the trees but they looked up as the pyramid was lit from above, on what must have been an important date, on a forgotten calendar, with no priest and no multitudes, only the scattered seekers who watched as if in a dream, with little connection to their past and no one knowing how to interact. The light split apart and performed a maneuver they would tell stories about for all of their days, the only meaning it would ever have. No one would be sacrificed. There would be no expectation placed on the maize as a result of their arrival. And if it weren't for the ones who held up their cell phones and emailed the videos to relatives who posted them to Facebook pages until they found their way to YouTube channels, no one else would have ever known. This moment wouldn't have existed. The return wouldn't have been documented.

"Buena suerte, turistas de las estrellas! Tourists of the stars!"

"We have nothing! We are nobodies!"

"Bring us good luck or be on thy way!"

Above Indiana, Airman Riley wasn't even sure he was seeing his mother's old house, and he became bored with sights he could have conjured himself simply by closing his eyes.

"Want to take it for a spin?" he said to the Major.

"Can I?"

"Clear your head and it will take you where you want to go."

The Major stepped forward and he placed his hand where Riley's had been. There were so many sites he'd been tasked with finding out about, but there was one in particular he didn't think his superiors were interested in pursuing, so he went there and he hovered above a dirt airstrip on a farm. The guy who wrote the letters in the sky at the conference lived there, and the Major wanted to know if the guy knew what it said. It wasn't long before he came out of his house and he took off in the yellow biplane. He flew in arcs and dives and he reproduced the letters from memory, and there was the UFO again in the sky.

When Arnie landed, the Major landed next to him, and he and the Airman came out to greet him.

"You ain't little green men after all," Arnie said.

And the Major said, "Do you think you could do that again? In one of these?"

Arnie understood what was being offered but honestly didn't know how to respond. "I could try," he said, and that was good enough. And he and the Airman and the Major went up again together in the saucer and Arnie was offered a new job right on the spot. He'd never believed in UFOs and here he was flying one.

Because Riley's heart wasn't in it, but Arnie's was, the Major said, "We would pay you very well to continue to do this."

"Why not?" he said. "Sounds fun."

When Cher sent off her book, which involved approving the contract with an e-signature, and emailing the final draft, she realized she hadn't asked the cosmos anything about herself. Was this book going to make her happy? Should she stop eating meat like Tommy? What did those letters in the sky mean, if they meant anything? And what had been going on with Tommy lately?

He was up early and getting ready to go teach. After the first couple of weeks he quit wearing suits but wore the same purple Polo and khakis, which was odd. He wouldn't have washed them, so she automatically did two small loads every night, because the purple and the khaki couldn't be washed together, and she washed anything else that could be thrown in with them, trying not to be wasteful. When she asked him about it, his answers were vague.

He said, "This I like," or "This is much happiness for me."

And so she let it go. But now she wished she hadn't, because with the book manuscript done she couldn't help but give in to the illogical idea that maybe the answers to the universe would be closed off to her, that she'd had a window of time, and it was shut. Maybe she wouldn't be able to return to that headspace. Or maybe wherever the answers came from, they had run dry.

She waited until Tommy left and she sat in the middle of the bed and she closed her eyes.

"Why is Tommy dressed like that?" she wanted to know, but her inquiry was met with silence.

"Tommy would never wear a purple Polo. Not on his life." She spoke aloud, which wasn't meditative, but she needed to know, so she persisted.

"Why is my Tommy in purple?" she said, and finally the answer came.

In her mind she heard the same voice that had given her the book, and with the same kind of simple yet wise reply it said, "He is in much happiness." And: "He will sell many things."

In the months after the conference, Arnie found he really missed the camaraderie. Strangers had listened to him and believed him. They'd asked earnest questions and they'd respected his point of view.

So when a large saucer appeared in the sky outside his window, he knew exactly what to do. He ran out of the house, he fired up his skywriter, and he took off into the air. He wrote the letters again, and when he landed, the saucer followed him and landed too.

There were two human men who came out of the craft, military types, and they offered to let him fly it. Which he did, splendidly. It was a dream machine and it responded exactly to his every command. The Major offered him a job, which he accepted, making him

Airman Arnie Fishman, and he was sworn in as a new member of the secret space force right there in his front yard.

Amy didn't tell Jim about her new hobby until her first story was published in *Interstellar Flight Terminal Departures Gate B Magazine.* When she showed him her contributor's copy, he was surprised. She wanted him to read it right there and then, but she was afraid of what he might think. Maybe she was crazy and this story would reveal it once and for all. He was also apprehensive because what if he was in her story and it showed what she really thought of him.

But he sat next to her on the couch and he read to himself as she fidgeted. Amy's story took place at the Ozarks Conference and it was about an erotonaut, which made him nervous. Because when he thought about the conference he remembered that he had been an erotonaut, and he wondered if maybe she knew. A part of him thought she didn't care – if she wasn't giving him hotel sex, she also couldn't be too upset or surprised when someone else did. Except that they were married, so of course she cared.

Then maybe this was about someone else, or something else, and he saw how it was supposed to be funny, though he was too self-conscious to laugh, and she sat next to him expecting him to laugh. And while he didn't laugh, he did say, "This is funny," and that was a big relief.

She said, "Oh, good. I was worried you wouldn't like it."

He hadn't really said that he liked it, though he understood how she might interpret him that way.

"Which parts were your favorites?" she said.

"I haven't finished," he said. "But so far all of them."

"What did you think was funny?"

And he had to be careful what he said because, while he knew his wife wasn't a racist, and he knew she wrote with good intentions, most of the story was centered around racial stereotypes, and he didn't want to appear to condone that kind of satire. What if he emboldened her and she went around telling people the parts she thought were funniest, but that were also possibly offensive, so that out of the context of the story she might come across as insensitive?

"I liked how this alien was here for fun," Jim said. "I think most of them are portrayed like robots, or too serious, or too business-like. This one was more like us."

"He is, isn't he? Though it's not like we go around dancing all the time, or having casual sex."

"He's like the seventies."

"I know!"

"It's like the seventies came from space."

"That's what *I* was thinking when I wrote it."

"It's *so* good."

"Really?"

"I really think so."

There was very little training, because they didn't know enough about the craft, but one thing the Major told Airman Arnie that really stuck was that a ship with it's own gravity can be a disturbance to the fabric of space-time.

"It can alter time?" Arnie asked.

"We don't know."

"It time travels?"

"It might."

"And this is good? This is bad?"

"It just is. But you should remain conscious of this fact. Every change can ripple changes around it. You can transform existence, or you can get stuck in a loop."

"And that's bad?"

"It might be bad. Are you ready to fly?"

"Where to?"

"Here's a list of locations to commit to memory," the Major said. "Find out what you can. You may not notice all that's happening, but with regression we can peel back the layers. There may be more going on than it seems."

"Regression?"

"We hypnotize you. We ask questions. To gain perspective."

"You do this?"

"We found a guy. He was at that conference. I didn't want to go, and look how fruitful it's been."

Arnie saluted the Major, which he enjoyed doing, but the Major looked at him like he wasn't supposed to, or like he'd done it wrong. Arnie walked up the ramp of light into the saucer, he went into the control room, he placed his hand on the six-fingered impression, and the saucer lifted off.

Above Indiana, in a nondescript neighborhood, he saw his friend Amy out in her backyard. The ship must have known he was remembering her and wondering about her, and so they flew there. Amy was with her husband and her neighbors. A column of smoke lifted high above them and they all looked up and pointed their cameras. Arnie had their attention and he wanted to say 'Hi,' so he flew in swoops and sharp angles to produce the symbols Amy had once commissioned him to write. And this ship was perfect for the job, these letters the best he'd done yet.

As Jim slept with the TV on, Amy worked on her latest story. She tried to remember the saucer she'd seen, so she could describe it, the precisely circular thing that had propelled them into all of this. Was it orange or silver? Her memory was confused. She also couldn't remember quite how large the ship was and she clicked over to

Messageinthesky.org to study Cher's picture, but the website was gone. She was redirected to Amyclinton.com, her author's website, with the only pictures the stock photos of fountain pens and unevenly stacked hardback books—and of course her author photo, the one Jim had taken of her in front of her favorite oak tree in exchange for sex. She wore a NASA t-shirt under a yellow cardigan and she wondered if she should have dressed more for church. But she wanted to look like a science-fiction writer and she supposed she did. She had Cher's picture somewhere on the hard drive but she couldn't remember what folder she'd put it in. It was unlike her not to remember.

A voice in her head said, "Go and see," and though the voice was inside, she knew the source was from somewhere outside that also lit up the yard and the windows and the hall beyond the bedroom.

She got up without fear and she walked down the hall to the kitchen to take a look. There it was taking up the whole backyard, hovering and bobbing, silver and glowing purple, a perfect saucer sixty feet across. She'd have no problem describing it now, though she was no longer interested in typing on her laptop.

She opened the patio door and went outside. She walked up a path of light and into the craft, which was a smooth metal, with clean lines and no ornamentation or signs of wear. Of all the things she couldn't remember, she *did* remember Christie Lewis telling her how to discern the real UFOs from the fakes; there was no dust in the illuminated air, no dirt on her bare feet. There was a short hall that led to an open door, where a room held her destiny. She was about to ascend and she didn't care if she ever came back. This was what was happening. This was what they had wanted to tell her.

卐 卐 卐

Acknowledgements

To all the students, who were the best teachers I've had.

About the Author

John Minichillo is the author of four small-press novels. He lives in Nashville and teaches at Tennessee State University.

About the Publishing Team

Nate Ragolia is a lifelong lover of science fiction and its power to imagine worlds more hopeful and inclusive than the real one. His first book, *There You Feel Free*, was published by 1888's Black Hill Press in 2015. Spaceboy Books reissued it in 2021. He's also the author of *The Retroactivist* (2017). His most recent book, *One Person Can't Make a Difference* (2022), was featured on Tor.com's Can't Miss Indie Press Speculative Fiction list, and was translated into Italian for Ringworld Sci-Fi in 2023. He founded and edited *BONED*, a literary magazine, and also created two webcomics. Nate is also a husband and a dog dad.

Shaunn Grulkowski has been compared to Warren Ellis and Phillip K. Dick and was once described as what a baby conceived by Kurt Vonnegut and Margaret Atwood would turn out to be. He's at least the fifth best Slavic-Latino-American sci-fi writer in the Baltimore metro area. He's the author *Retcontinuum*, and the editor of *A Stalled Ox* and *The Goldfish* for 1888/Black Hill Press.